Freestyle

By Monica S. Baker

Schiffer Publishing Ltd®

4880 Lower Valley Road   Atglen, Pennsylvania   19310

Other Schiffer Books on Related Subjects:
Autumn Journey, 978-0-87033-606-5, $12.95
Grandfather's Secret, 978-0-7643-3535-8, $12.99
Leonard Calvert and the Maryland Adventure, 978-0-87033-502-0, $9.95
Oyster Moon, 978-0-87033-459-7, $9.95
Secret of Belle Meadow, 978-0-87033-554-9, $9.95

Library of Congress Control Number: 2010925951

Cover designed by Bruce Waters
Type set in Minion Pro

ISBN: 978-0-7643-3538-9
Printed in The United States of America

Schiffer Books are available at special discounts for bulk purchases for sales promotions or premiums. Special editions, including personalized covers, corporate imprints, and excerpts can be created in large quantities for special needs. For more information contact the publisher:

Published by Schiffer Publishing Ltd.
4880 Lower Valley Road
Atglen, PA 19310
Phone: (610) 593-1777; Fax: (610) 593-2002
E-mail: Info@schifferbooks.com

For the largest selection of fine reference books on this and related subjects, please visit our web site
at **www.schifferbooks.com**
We are always looking for people to write books on new and related subjects. If you have an idea for
a book please contact us at the above address.

This book may be purchased from the publisher.
Include $5.00 for shipping.
Please try your bookstore first.
You may write for a free catalog.

In Europe, Schiffer books are distributed by
Bushwood Books
6 Marksbury Ave.
Kew Gardens
Surrey TW9 4JF England
Phone: 44 (0) 20 8392 8585; Fax: 44 (0) 20 8392 9876
E-mail: info@bushwoodbooks.co.uk
Website: www.bushwoodbooks.co.uk

Dedication

To George. Freedom Awaits.

"What is past, is prologue."

-William Shakespeare

DEAD: Patty Cannon, Notorious Kidnapper and Murderess, Somewhere of 50 – 60 years of age

Sussex County, Delaware—The flagrantly wicked and mostly evil Patty Cannon took her own life yesterday in the Sussex County jail whilst waiting to be hanged in the gallows of the Georgetown, Delaware square. Crafty and sly, the Cannon wench consumed a thickly poison from a glass vial that she had sewn into the hem of her skirt. Always the killer and never the killed, Patty Cannon thus stole from the sheriff the honor of having a hand in her much anticipated and deserved death.

May Pirate Patty never rest in peace.

Chapter 1

Sunday Night. In the Meadow.

Mitch shut his tired eyes and curled his long fingers over his sheets. The day's obituaries crinkled under his pillow. "I hate my life."

DEAD: Mitchell Thomas Burke: Loser, Age 13

The clock clicked to 11:59 P.M. and he inhaled. On his exhale he whispered, "Dear God, please take care of Dad."

One one thousand, two one thousand...

"And, please let me dream about the meadow."

...three one thousand, four one thousand...

"I can do what I want there."

...five one thousand, six one thousand...

At 12:01 A.M., he fell into a deep sleep, which lifted him to the middle of a sparkling summer meadow.

"Mitchey, Mitchey-boy! Do you see fit to play? Do you want to play a new game?"

Mitch opened his eyes.

The creek on the edge of the field gurgled, and a tall woman wearing a grey linen skirt to her ankles gathered sticks under a towering black ash tree. A comfortable heat rolled over Mitch's lanky body as the sun swirled in the sky. He ran all ten fingers through his dark brown hair. The meadow was perfect. No rain, no poison ivy, and no mosquitoes. To Mitch, it smelled like his mother's favorite bubble bath.

"Come along, boy. Time's a wasting," the woman called from across the meadow.

Mitch sat up and watched her stroll from the tree, through the tall sweeping grass, to a thick jumble of thorny bushes that lined the woods. She was a large woman with a fair, but ruddy, complexion, blue-black hair, and strong shoulders and hands. Mitch guessed her to be in her fifties or sixties.

"Hello, Patty!" he called.

She whistled through her fingers and Josiah appeared. Creeping out of the dense woods and sticky brambles, Josiah went to Patty's side. The cocoa-skinned boy came no higher than her waist and wore a beige muslin shirt and loose pants, which were probably made from a flour sack. His soft brown curls carpeted his head like moss on a river stone.

Patty turned, cradling the craggy sticks in one arm and holding up her skirt with the other, and headed back across the meadow toward Mitch. Her stride was long and sure, and Josiah stumbled and ran to keep up with her.

"Mitchey boy!" she called well before she reached him. "We're going to play a game of quick reaction."

Patty had first commandeered Mitch's dreams earlier in the summer, soon after his father's Navy reserve unit shipped out to war in the Middle East. He'd been sleeping fitfully that night—twisting in his sheets—when she had nudged the back of his shoulder blade with a sharp, whittled stick.

"Boy!" she called. "You've got some learning to do!"

Mitch didn't know what to make of her. She moved like a man, but spoke like a lady.

"I can see you're timid. You've many strengths and you're a bright one, but your weaknesses overshadow the strong points. You're a worrier, and you need some skills. I'm here to help you." She buddy-slapped his back with her massive hands. "Let's work out the strong bits. Sharpen them, so to speak." Mitch soon came to enjoy her attention.

Patty now planted her feet wide on the ground before her charge. The familiar smell of linen washed with harsh lye soap overshadowed the smell of bubble bath in the meadow. "Get up, boy."

"Sure!" Mitch jumped to his feet, dusted himself off, and inspected his own loose trousers, muslin shirt, and thick rope belt. No zippers or buttons to worry about. He looked behind Patty's imposing figure and smiled. "Hello, Josiah."

Josiah glanced first at Patty, then at Mitch. "'Lo, Mitch," he mumbled. When Patty winked at him, Josiah shifted his gaze to his own muddy and calloused bare feet.

"Weren't we going to learn to shoot a gun today?" Mitch pointed to the black pistol hitched to the tooled leather belt on Patty's hips. Shooting a gun was not an opportunity his mother allowed in his 21st century waking life.

"Nah. I think this parlor game would be a tad more fun for today." She fixed her large hands on Mitch's broad shoulders and positioned him at Josiah's side. Next to Mitch, Josiah appeared taller and rose as high as Mitch's collarbone. They both waited for Patty to speak.

"Now then, let's play Pigeon Flies. Sit down there in the short grass." She pointed to the matted spot on the ground with the largest and crustiest switch from her pile, its bark flaking off its wood.

The boys sat down cross-legged, Mitch quicker and more eager than Josiah. Patty sat before them and easily folded her long, sturdy legs cross-legged herself, exposing only her white, thick muscled calves from under the hem of her skirt.

"Both of you put your pointer finger on my knee here." She flicked an ant from the skirt over her knee and replaced it with her own finger. "When I holler the name of an animal that flies, like a pigeon, you raise your finger to the sky." Patty raised her finger high above her head. "If you don't raise your finger, or if you raise your finger when I call an animal that doesn't fly, you forfeit."

"You mean we lose?" asked Mitch.

"That would be correct." Patty lifted the switch and laid it straight across her lap, its sharp tip pointing at Mitch's chest. She brushed her hair off her sweaty forehead. "As I'm the leader and there's only the two of you, this game will pass quickly. Think carefully and act fast to win."

Mitch shifted on his rear until he was comfortable, happily awaiting the start of the game. Josiah hadn't moved since he settled in the grass, and now purposely and slowly closed his eyes.

Patty sat tall, her shoulders straight and rigid as the switch across her lap. "Get ready," she said.

Josiah opened his eyes and the boys each put a forefinger on her knee, Mitch's white finger touching Josiah's brown.

"Wasp!"

The game began. Two fingers flew into the air and then back to Patty's knee. As soon as the fingers landed, she called "bluebird," and the fingers again flew upward.

"Cat!"

Without looking at each other, both boys kept their pulsing fingers on her knee.

"Pigeon!"

Up shot the fingers, as if they were strung together with invisible fishing line. Mitch grinned and sat up even straighter; bolts of energy surged up his spine with each call from Patty.

"Mosquito!"

I hate mosquitoes, thought Mitch.

Two fingers went up again, and then down in anticipation of the next call. Mitch glanced over and saw Josiah's eyes focused on the black faded patch hand-stitched on the hem of Patty's skirt.

"Beetle!" Patty called.

Josiah jutted his finger up above his head. Mitch hesitated.

Beetles crawl on the ground.

He pressed his finger deep into Patty's square knee, and not into the air.

Patty eyed Josiah's finger in the air, and then Mitch's on her knee. Grinning, she rolled the switch on her lap, and then raised it.

WHACK!

The weapon smashed across Mitch's neck, sending him crumbling to his side. "Argh! What are you doing?" He grabbed his neck and rolled from shoulder to shoulder, as if he could rock the pain away.

The large woman pushed herself up off the ground with a grunt, smoothed her skirt, and loomed over Mitch, casting a chilly shadow on his face. He rubbed his neck with both hands while holding back his tears.

"In the meadow," Patty said as she strode a circle around him, "our beetles don't crawl, they fly."

Chapter 2

Monday Morning.

"I didn't know that!" Mitch cried from his bed.

"Mitchell, are you okay?" Mrs. Burke peeked in the open door to her son's bedroom. Darkness cloaked the room, except for morning's pink blush, which was sneaking through the window blinds. Mitch, not quite awake, hugged the blanket and sheet to his naked chest and scanned the room for Patty and Josiah. His brown eyes floated under a watery glaze.

"Oh, dear," the petite Mrs. Burke whispered over the click of her heels on the hardwood floor. "You're having another nightmare." She sat on the side of Mitch's twin bed and rubbed his back. "You haven't had one of those all summer."

Mitch "pulled it together," as his sister Annie called the act of pretending you're over something, when deep down you're not. He rolled the covers to his lap and sat up in bed. "I'm okay, Mom. Just a dream." He rubbed his eyes with the palms of his hands.

What happened?

"You didn't dream about those obituaries, did you, Baby?"

Mitch clutched the remaining sheet to his chin and turned to face the creamy white wall. "I don't remember what the dream was about," he lied. "And, I'm not a baby."

"Well, if you remember your nightmare, let me know." His mother held her hair behind one ear, leaned over, and kissed his forehead. Her gold Italian crucifix fluttered against his cheek, as if Jesus were trying to peck him, too.

"Why don't you come on downstairs and have breakfast with me? I've got half an hour before I go to work." She left, leaving the door open behind her.

Mitch slid out of bed, pulling the crinkled obituaries from under his pillow. He stumbled to the hall bathroom in his boxer shorts and tossed the newspaper in the garbage. Standing in front of the toilet, he faced the mirror his mom had placed behind it in a moment of decorating frenzy. He raised the toilet seat before he relieved himself and looked at his own sleepy face.

Why did Patty hit me?

While Mitch's face still slept, his body woke to the morning. He rolled his shoulders so that his collarbone subtly protruded from his tanned chest—the sign of a swimmer's body surging deeper into adolescence. From the collarbone rose his defined neck, and on his neck rose a bruise shaped like a tree switch. Mitch touched it.

She never laid a hand on me before.

He inspected the new growth of soft hair under his arms, finished peeing, but didn't flush—a habit he had got into so he wouldn't wake Annie. Mitch washed his hands, donned a white T-shirt to conceal his underarm hair, and quietly descended the stairs to meet his mom in the kitchen. The wall clock above the sink was shaped like a rooster, its tail ticking off the seconds.

"Look," she said, smiling over her bowl of raisin bran, "a present. No need to hide them under your pillow anymore." She slid the open obituary section across the table to Mitch, her charm bracelet clanking like dog tags.

"Very funny, Mom." He sat on the oak chair across from her and focused on the columns of words in front of him. Most entries were accompanied by either a bad, okay, or good, but never great, black-and-white photo of the recently deceased—the very dead. Every so often, a grainy color photo popped off the page.

"Why do you read those every day?"

"You've asked me this a million times," he said while scanning the columns. His eyes settled on a photo of a serious young man dressed in military whites. He memorized the lines of the face.

"Try me again. I'm still not sure I understand why a rising eighth grader needs to read about strangers' deaths. Why can't you stop worrying about dead people and get out with your friends, or something?"

"I'm reading about interesting people, not strangers." Mitch sighed. "And, you know perfectly well my friends go on vacation in August."

Besides, I have Patty. Patty is good company. Usually.

He massaged his neck with one hand as he tried to read about the young soldier. The bruise had risen to a small, warm welt, so he tugged at his T-shirt collar to cover it.

Mitch's mom snatched the paper from him and opened it over her cereal bowl.

"Mom!"

"Hmm. Let's see. Here it reads, 'June Olney, accountant, in her sleep on July 30.'" She returned the wadded paper to her son. "Frankly, she doesn't sound interesting to me."

"How can you say that?" Mitch clutched the paper to his chest.

"Don't get so worked-up about it. It's not that big a deal." She stood to put the gallon of milk in the refrigerator and then grabbed her car keys from the windowsill over the sink.

"It is to Mrs. Olney's family. How would you like it if people made fun of your obituary?"

"Come on, Mitchell."

"Or, Dad's?"

His mother spun from the sink to face Mitch nose-to-nose. "Don't you ever mention 'Dad' and 'obituary' in the same sentence, young man. Do you hear me?"

Bad move.

"I'm sorry, Mom." He fingered the folded newspaper on the table. "You know I didn't mean that about Dad."

She sighed, "Forget it." Slowly, she picked up her purse, the size of a brown paper grocery bag, and slung it over her shoulder. "Look, I've gotta run to work. Remember, when your sister wakes up, ride your bikes to swim team and come home by eleven. I'll call to see that you're here." She sailed through the side door with Mitch drafting behind her.

Barefoot, he hopped across the piercing gravel as his mother crunched ahead and climbed into the blue minivan. "Mom?" he yelled. "I hate swim team. The swimsuit…"

"I'm not going over that again with you, Mitchell," she replied out of the car window. "Now, go clean your room before practice. And, pick your summer essay topic. School starts in two weeks!" She put the car in reverse.

Right.

"Bye, honey!"

Her words hung in the air, but not in Mitch's head. He ran his fingers through his thick hair.

This day stinks already.

At least his summer essay was covered. Most of the information Mitch needed was in an old *National Geographic* magazine he'd found in his dad's den. The entire edition was devoted to the Underground Railroad, one of his assigned essay choices. He had already started reading the article and taking notes. His summer essay was born.

Mitch drew a circle with his toe in the dusty gravel. The morning was hot and muggy, much like a normal August morning in Clean Drinking, Maryland. The neighborhood was quiet, except for the neighbor's overly confident dachshund, Fritzi, whose yaps could be heard from inside the Burke's house.

Instinctively, he massaged his neck again and turned away from the main road and toward his home. Eyeing a smooth stone the size of a dime, he picked it up from the driveway and popped it at the siding of the house. Immediately, the door flew open as if the house itself had suffered a reflex reaction. "I'm telling Mom you're throwing rocks at the house!" Annie screeched from the steps.

"Shut-up!" Mitch yelled back.

"I'm telling Mom you said shut-up!"

Mitch tossed another stone at the steps.

Annie was adopted when Mitch was two and too young to object. They had grown together like blood siblings, and the only reminders of Annie's adopted status was her oyster pearl skin and sky-blue eyes, which stood out in a household of olive complexions and brown eyes.

She stared at her brother as she pulled the clips, one at a time, out of her bun, letting her blond hair collapse on her shoulders. "Shut-up is for the dog. I'm going to tell Dad, too!" Her round face landed in a pout.

"We don't have a dog!" Mitch shouted back. "And, Dad's not even here." He dropped his stones and hobbled back across the gravel towards the open door.

Watching him advance, Annie tightened the belt on her pink fuzzy robe. "He can still answer e-mail." She stuck out her tongue, using her entire upper body to support the launch forward.

Mitch bumped against her as he entered the house. "We have to bike to swim practice today. Get ready."

"What's the matter? Did your two armpit hairs fall out?"

I wish Dad were home.

The Defense Department just announced that certain Reserves would be staying in the Middle East longer than planned. In fact, Mr. Thomas Burke might not be coming home this month after all.

Ignoring his sister, Mitch trudged up the stairs to the second floor, the facial lines and smile of the young man in the obituaries planted in his head.

The obituary said he was buried in Arlington National Cemetery.

Annie followed him up the stairs and down the hall to his bedroom. "Mitch, why are you so cranky every morning? And, how's your girlfriend?"

DEAD: Anna Maria Burke, Bratty Sister, Age 11

"She's not a girlfriend, and she's probably old enough to be our grandma. Could you get ready for swim team and leave me alone?" He yanked the laundry basket from his closet. "I shouldn't have told you about Patty at all."

Annie plopped herself on Mitch's stripped bed. "Why do they call it a twin bed when it's the only one?" she said, flipping her hair back into a messy bun at the nape of her neck.

"Go away." He scooped a dirty T-shirt from the floor and lobbed it into the laundry basket.

"I know…you've been thinking about death and dying again." Annie flopped backwards and pointed her feet to the ceiling, her eyes on her glittery green toenails. "Jeez Mitch, don't you get enough of that in Sister Maureen Anne's religion class?"

"Get off the bed so I can make it."

Annie tumbled off the bed and onto the blanket puddled on the floor, wrapping herself in it like the pigs in a blanket sold at the county fair. "Look!" She threw her arms over her head and rolled.

"Oh, God," Mitch pulled his lycra swim trunks from his top dresser drawer. "I hope this day goes by fast."

"You're using the Lord's name in vain."

"Whatever."

"All you care about is that lady in your dreams. Patty, Patty, Patty!"

"I told you about her in confidence. Stop it, or I'll knock you one!" He threw his trunks at her face, aiming to hurt.

Annie caught the trunks and laughed until her bun escaped its clips. "You, Mitchell Burke, couldn't hurt a bug!"

Chapter 3
Monday Afternoon. In the library.

When Mitch's father left for active duty in the Middle East, his mother, with a rather nervy reflex, re-enlisted Mitch to swim with the Ladybugs, their local swim team.

At the age of six, Mitch had been enthralled with the free hot dogs offered to swimmers on meet nights and begged to join the team. From seven to nine, he had happily competed in the Ladybug swim trunks. At ten, the girly-cute bug logo on the trunk legs had begun to embarrass him. At eleven, the lycra trunks themselves had become a problem, as he noticed them awkwardly hugging his private parts. At 12, the lycra effect totally mortified Mitch and he pleaded the end of his swimming career with his dad. After last summer, he thought he'd hung up his Ladybug trunks forever.

And then his father left for war.

During a miserably long swim practice, Mitch and Annie swam six lanes apart in the pool, the water and other Ladybugs cushioning the tension between them. Afterwards, Annie placed a pleading phone call to her mother, gained escape approval, and wedged her bike in the back of the Mulbry family's small station wagon, setting out with her best friend Meghan and Mrs. Mulbry to their house on the west side of town.

Mitch was on his own for the day. He eagerly left the pool and biked directly to the library to use the Internet. While their dad was away, Mrs. Burke cut the service to the house earlier in the summer, fearing unsupervised access would corrupt her children. Mitch was now totally and painfully dependent on the library's system.

After a peaceful ride, he parked his bike by the library front door. The yellow button to the automatic handicapped-friendly door jammed, so Mitch heaved the glass door open with both hands and walked into the lobby. The Clean Drinking Library was the oldest and smallest of the libraries in the county system, but it boasted air conditioning and the Internet. He turned left in the cool air and headed to the polished wooden information desk, where he cautiously greeted the senior library volunteer.

"Excuse me, ma'am. May I use a computer?"

The volunteer, a middle-aged to very old lady, made sure that no one, not any living creature, could log onto the Internet for more than 20 minutes. Reluctantly, she penciled-in Mitch's name on her crisp yellow sign-in sheet and reminded him of her imposed limit.

He found his computer and sat, feeling the volunteer's gaze puncture each vertebrae of his spine, starting at his neck and ending at his tail. He shifted in his seat, logged on, gathered his thoughts, and stretched his fingers. Finally, he clicked open his email account, Free_Style@aol.com, and began a message to his dad.

Hi Dad, what's up? The brat is at a friend's house and Mom's at work. So, how are you?

Mitch stopped to ponder his note.

Anyway, Mom's on my case again. She's all stressed out with work and with us and is ordering me around. It stinks. And, I had a kind of nightmare last night.

He sat back and rubbed the receding welt on his neck.

I can't send that to Dad…the Reserve Family Readiness people told us to be strong for Dad and not to worry him.

In the meeting his family attended at the old high school gym before his dad deployed, the military's Family Readiness people were friendly and served chocolate chip cookies, but didn't answer a lot of Mitch's questions like, "When is my Dad coming home?" Instead, they told him to be brave.

Bad news can distract soldiers in combat.

Click. Double click.

Mitch deleted the last part of the message and started over.

Anyway, I swam ok in practice this morning, but I'm sick of the stupid swim trunks. They show everything and Mom doesn't get it … since she's a girl, you know. I'm definitely not swimming next summer. Especially on a team named the Ladybugs. I know it's called that for good luck and everything, but give me a break! It's not like when I was a little kid. I hate it now.

I hope you're safe. Mitch

p.s. Do all beetles fly?

"Time's up!"

Click.

Mitch hit the "send" button before the old lady could order him off the computer.

DEAD: Library Lady, Crabby Volunteer, Age 186

He logged off, snuck out of the library without passing her desk, and biked the two miles home. There, he luxuriated in peace and quiet. Sitting in his father's den, he read some of the *National Geographic* and four back issues of the *Cosmic Comic* books. He showered in peace, heated and ate a frozen burrito in peace, and, when his mother came home late from picking up Annie, managed to chat briefly with her and ignore his sister at the same time.

"Guys, I'm tired. Lights out." After ten o'clock, Mrs. Burke flipped the hallway switch and padded to her bedroom, a tired-out Annie following to her own room.

Mitch settled in his bed without complaining, turned out the light, rolled over on his side, and touched his neck. The welt had almost completely disappeared.

Patty will be here soon.

He exhaled slowly.

I can ask why she hit me.

He inhaled again. "Dear God, please keep Dad safe." On the steady exhale, he fell asleep.

Chapter 4

Monday Night. The Meadow, Again.

"Mitchey-boy, wake up."

Mitch opened his eyes to see Patty, pacing in a circle on the meadow ground around him. Josiah still sat cross-legged across from him, stroking a shiny black beetle in the palm of his hand, his eyes focused on the grass he sat on. The beetle's relatives buzzed in harmony in the distance.

"Hey!" Mitch pushed himself up to a sitting position and touched the bulging memory on his neck.

"Why, why did you hit me?"

Patty continued her stroll, drawing a line in the dry ground with her switch. "Now that tap didn't hurt you that much, did it? Strong boy like you?"

"Well, a bit." Mitch dropped his hand to his side.

"I've been telling you. You've got some learning to do."

"But I thought beetles only crawl."

She stopped circling and stepped toward Josiah, pointing her switch to the bug in his hand. "Not everything is what it seems. People, even critters, can conceal just about anything from anybody. Look at this beetle here. Josiah, show Mitchey what this heavy, ugly bug can do."

Josiah folded his fingers around the beetle and slowly stood up. He extended his arm in front of him, opened his fingers and, with his other hand, cleared the beetle off his palm. As if on cue, the bug released a pair of hidden, transparent wings and buzzed above Josiah's head.

"See that?" Patty pointed to the flying beetle. "Never underestimate anybody, anything." She swished the switch at her side, and then tapped Josiah on the shoulder. "Now both of you close your eyes."

Mitch watched Josiah hesitantly close his watery eyes and, against his better judgment, closed his own eyes.

WHACK!

Chapter 5
Tuesday Morning. The Rude Awakening.

Mitch slowly settled in at the kitchen table, the rooster tail clicking and clocking its morning greeting.

Oh, my God. That was so weird.

Mrs. Burke had already rested a full plate at his place. "Sorry for dragging you out of bed. But, I need to go over the day before I leave."

He stared at his waffles, waking to the moment.

Click. Clock.

Patty didn't hit Josiah, did she?

His jittery fingers touched the obituaries that rested in their new spot—by his plate. He circled a photo of a smiling old man.

"Okay, let's talk about your day." Mrs. Burke stood with the wall calendar in her hand and continued, "You've got swim team and then you're in charge of Annie until I get home."

His fingers rested on the old gentleman's face. "Annie is fine without me."

His mom turned away from the table and pronounced, "Today. Summer essay topic." She tapped the counter with her forefinger. "You have got to start making some progress on this, or…"

"But that's what I want to do today! I need to spend the day in the library. Alone." He smoothed his tussled hair with both hands, subtly slipping his right hand to his neck. The welt was gone.

"Nope. You can hit the library tomorrow." She efficiently said her piece and left the kitchen.

"Why not today?" Mitch followed her to the door. "I'll watch the brat another day."

"Nope." Mrs. Burke opened the door and turned to Mitch. "And, don't call your sister a brat. Bye, hon." She exited and shut the door behind her.

Mitch kicked the closed door with his right bare foot.

"Damn!"

"Oh, Mitchell…" Annie's voice cascaded down the stairs, like the trickle before a flood. "I'm telling Mom you swore!" She peeked around the corner and then glided into the kitchen.

"Go ahead," Mitch said. He rubbed his toes and hobbled to the table.

Annie helped herself to two waffles and sat across from her brother, who was trying to concentrate on the obituaries. A Mr. Henry Smithworth's obituary was running prominently for the third day in a row, a sure sign his family had money to spend. Mitch flipped the page.

No soldiers today. No reservists.

Annie eyed his newspaper and said, "I have a great idea for today!" She scooted up on her knees in her chair and leaned across the table into her brother. "Let's play hooky from swim practice and go on a hike down by the spring!" She sat back on her heels and thrust a three-layer waffle bite past, but not completely over, her lips. Thick brown syrup trickled down her chin. "Mom will never know." Waffle oozed out of her smile.

"No way. Mom will find out and *I'll* get in trouble, not you, the little princess."

"She'll never know. The entire neighborhood is away on vacation, and Mom never talks with our coach. Today is the perfect day." Annie took her last inhalation of waffle and picked up the plate with both hands to lick it.

"That's gross." Mitch reached across the table and stopped her before her protruding tongue hit the plate.

"Come on." She hopped off her chair and pulled one knee up to her chest like a sleeping flamingo. "We can just hang out at the creek. No one will bother us. I'll even show you where I found the deer skeleton."

"But you said you made up the story about the skeleton."

She dropped her knee. "Nope. I made up the story that I made up the story about the skeleton. I don't want the entire neighborhood messing with the bones." She skated across the floor in her sock feet, from one end of the kitchen to the other, until she slowed down and stopped in front of Mitch's seat. "Look." She thought for about half of a second. "I won't tell Mom about your nightmare with Patty last night."

"How do you know I had a nightmare?"

"Simple. I heard you scream." Annie cocked her head. "Twice." She skated on.

Chapter 6

Tuesday Afternoon. Oh, My God.

After another round of waffles, Mitch successfully negotiated his idea of a safe hooky day with Annie. They would skip swim team practice, but stay behind closed doors and drawn curtains playing Annie's favorite *Masher* video game and watching TV together until noon, when they would normally arrive home from the pool. Then, Mitch would work on his summer essay and Annie could do whatever she liked in the confines of the neighborhood. In return, Annie would keep Patty a secret from his mother.

The plan was a safe one, and after a lunch of peanut butter and banana sandwiches, Mitch's bartered hooky sentence was almost over.

Annie stood from the table and saluted Mitch. "It's not like you've been the best company in the world, but you may study now." She sock-skated around the corner and went up the stairs to her room. The boom-box blared pop music the second she entered her domain.

Mitch shook his head and poured another mug of milk. He pulled a pad of lined paper and a pencil from a kitchen drawer and walked to his dad's dark and cozy den, where the *National Geographic* magazine sat on the coffee table. A smoky blue and pink watercolor illustration of an escaping slave family wrapped in scarves and rags stared at him from the cover. He picked up the magazine, dropped into his favorite chair and draped his legs over the cracked leather rolled arms. It was his dad's favorite chair too.

Mitch smiled at that thought and carefully opened the musty 19-year-old magazine, removing the piece of toilet paper he left as a bookmark. First, he scanned the pictures, stopping at a yellowed 19th century reward poster on the right page. It began:

$200 Reward.

Runaway from the subscriber, last night, a mulatto man named FRANK MULLEN, about 21 years old, five feet ten or eleven inches high...

As he has absconded without any provocation, it is presumed he will make for Pennsylvania or New York. I will give one hundred dollars if taken in the State of Maryland, or the above reward if taken any where east of that State...

October 21, 1835   Thomas C. Scott

On the left page was a black and white photo of a Quaker businessman named Thomas Garrett. Garrett, an abolitionist in Wilmington, Delaware, spent 40 years leading fugitive slaves to freedom. The picture was of an older Garrett, taken after a lifetime of work. It showed a confidant man in a black top coat, sitting in a chair and looking directly into the camera. White hair softly framed the lined face of a comfortable man who had nothing to hide.

Mitch turned to the next page.

A full-page modern photo showed a sprawling white mansion built by slaves on a 2,500-acre Louisiana sugarcane plantation.

What a house. It looks like a hotel.

The opposite photo showed the crumbling wooden cabins the slaves lived in.

God.

Mitch sunk deeper into his seat to pick up where he'd left off the day before. The paragraph began with a discussion of Baltimore, Maryland, and its importance as a major junction on the Underground Railroad. Frederick Douglass, the famous fugitive slave who became a statesman, worked as a slave to a shipbuilder in Baltimore.

The author of the article wrote about his own visits to Cambridge, Maryland, not far from where the famous Harriet Tubman was born—on the opposite side of the expansive Chesapeake Bay from Baltimore. He followed the famous Underground Railroad conductor's tracks and "explored the crooked creeks of the Eastern Shore" of Maryland.

Wow. That's not far from here.

Harriet's route took her along the meandering Choptank River and its marshy inlets. The author described the area as "perilous country, home ground of the slave hunter Patty Cannon and her merciless gang."

"Wait. What?!" Mitch swung his legs off the arm of the chair and sat up straight. A chill socked the side of his neck and the hair rose on his arms.

Didn't Josiah call Patty 'Missus Cannon' in one of my dreams?

His heart pounded one huge thump. The telephone rang in the kitchen, but he didn't move to answer it.

Is my Patty, Patty Cannon?

"A tall, striking woman whose salty language was her trademark, Mrs. Cannon ran her underground railroad in reverse. A letter to Philadelphia Mayor Joseph Harris in 1826 suggests that her gang was abducting blacks as far north as his city."

Her gang? Is that what she meant when she told me she "had boys?"

"Sometimes she employed renegade blacks to entice fugitives into their homes as false station stops on the Underground Railroad. There the trusting runaways were entrapped by Patty's gang, who often tortured and murdered free blacks as well as escaped slaves and sold the survivors."

"Tortured?!" Mitch blurted out loud.

The pulse in Mitch's neck pushed rapidly through his skin. His shaking hands held the magazine close to his face.

"Finally captured and indicted for the murder of four fugitives—two of them children—Patty Cannon poisoned herself on May 11, 1829, in her prison cell at Georgetown, Delaware, cheating a public eager to witness her trial and execution."

"She murdered kids!"

The author of the magazine article went on to describe his own family's fascination with Patty, and his slave ancestors' fright at the mention of the horrible woman's name. Mitch couldn't read another line.

"Slave kidnapper Patty Cannon is coming to me in my dreams," he whispered.

He couldn't move.

BOOM. BOOM.

Annie bounded down the stairs. "Mitch! Mitch!" she wailed, running into the den. "The coach called! He's really angry!" She stopped in front of Mitch's chair. "We missed the *meet* practice! We forgot the make-up meet is tomorrow night!"

Mitch looked right through his sister.

What if she whacked Josiah and not the beetle?

"Remember? Last week's meet was rained out."

He threw his head into his hands and rocked in the chair. "Oh, my God. Oh, my GOD!"

Annie stepped back. "It's not that big of a deal, Mitch. We just need to make sure Mom doesn't find out we missed practice. We can't let her talk to the coach at the meet." She paused and put her hands on her hips. "And, you're not supposed to use God's name in vain. At least say, 'Dear God' so He'll think you're praying and not swearing."

"I feel sick." Mitch hurried to the guest bathroom and shut the door.

Chapter 7
Tuesday Evening.

Mitch sat on the toilet, with his head between his legs for over an hour. Annie checked on him periodically, pounding on the door and asking, "You okay, Mitch?" Each time she waited for an answer, her ear to the door, before she walked away.

"Uh-huh," was all the answer Mitch could muster.

But it was enough for Annie. On her last visit to the closed door she said, "Don't worry, Mitch. I'll take care of Mom. She'll never know we played hooky."

When he unfrazzled his nerves and knew Annie was far from the bathroom, Mitch opened the door and dashed up the stairs to his own bedroom. Solitude was necessary and he found it on his bed, where he lay on his back, staring at the plaster ceiling.

Don't close your eyes.

Patty's smiling face bobbed through his mind.

She killed people.

He shook his legs on the bed, trying to kick the anxiety out of his system.

Maybe it's not true. Maybe the magazine is wrong…this can't be true. This has to be about a different Patty.

A tingle spread around the base of his neck. He knew better.

Downstairs, Mrs. Burke came home from work and was chatting with Annie. The high pitch of his sister's patter carried upstairs, as did his mother's laugh.

"Dear God, please keep Mom downstairs."

BOOM. BOOM.

The walls vibrated as Annie scaled two steps at a time to Mitch's room, where she opened the door and pulled a dry hotdog in a crusty bun out of her pocket. "Mitch," Annie whispered. "The coast is clear. Mom doesn't suspect a thing."

Mitch dragged a pillow over his face.

"Come on, Mitch. Pull it together. You're off the hook. I told Mom you worked out so incredibly hard today that you're sore, tired, and in bed. She thinks you're sleeping."

"You told her another lie?" Mitch's muffled words emerged from his pillow.

Annie sighed. "You won't see Mom until the meet tomorrow. She's leaving for work early in the morning. She'll *never* know." Annie left the hotdog on his dresser and quietly shut the door.

"Thanks, Annie."

Mitch gulped the cold hotdog and then stared at the ceiling for two long hours, his head against the mattress, and pillow against his chest.

DEAD: Mitchell Thomas Burke, killed by a slave kidnapper in his dreams, Age 13

He listened to the buzz of his mom's and Annie's voices, and then the louder buzz of the TV blaring reality shows. He heard Annie say good night, and then his mother grind the coffee for the morning. The smell of crushed coffee beans floated all the way up the stairs. Time for bed.

What can I do? I can't go to sleep.

He clutched his pillow and rolled on his side. From that vantage point, he eyed the *Cosmic Comic* book collection he had piled on the floor.

I've got to do something to stay awake.

Quietly, Mitch slid off his bed so his mother wouldn't hear the squeak of the bed frame. Sitting cross-legged on his carpet, his back against his red beanbag chair, he carefully began to order the comics by number. The monotony of the project calmed him, and after ordering three sets of ten books, Mitch slumped into the beanbag chair, his chin on his chest, and fell asleep.

WHACK!

Chapter 8
Tuesday Night. It's True!

Still sitting, Mitch stared up at Patty, who stood over him in the hot, sticky meadow. Josiah sat huddled in the grass, his hands crossed over his head. A squashed beetle lay on the beaten ground.

"Josiah!" Mitch caught his breath. "She's a murderer!"

"I'm taking you. You're mine."

"What?" Mitch scurried backwards on his hands.

Patty took one large step towards Mitch. "I'm telling you that I'm taking you as mine."

The scorching sun beat down on Mitch's face. He looked at Josiah, still huddling with his hands on his head, dark sweat stains creeping from his armpits to his sides in dripping "V" formations. Then, he turned to Patty. "You, you're Patty Cannon!" Mitch clumsily stood to face her.

"I like you, boy. You might want to call me Pirate Patty." She clenched two tree switches in her right hand and leaned over to pick up the other sticks she had piled on the ground. "My friends call me that."

Mitch could smell her body odor. "But you, you killed people!" He pointed at Patty. "You're evil!"

Patty ambled towards trembling Josiah. "Now, now," she purred to Mitch. "Cool your temper. I'm not all that bad." She rubbed Josiah's head until he took his hands down. "I let Josiah here live, didn't I, boy?"

Josiah nodded his head up and down, but remained silent. His shaking hands rested on his knobby knees and he stared into the safety of the shaded woods, avoiding eye contact with either Mitch or Patty.

Why didn't I see that before? Josiah is afraid of her.

"And he can live, as long as he stays in my meadow." Patty jabbed Josiah with the switch. "Isn't that so, boy?"

Pearls of sweat tumbled down Josiah's brown brow. He nodded.

Mitch looked at the dead beetle and felt his own sweat more than he ever had on the hottest day in Clean Drinking. The beetle's glossy black armor was crushed flat against the canvas of its soft yellow guts. The once deceiving transparent wings had separated from the beetle's body and now jutted in opposite directions from each other in the dirt. Mitch swallowed. "But, you wouldn't kill Josiah, would you?"

"Killing doesn't bother me. It's getting rid of the body that's difficult." Patty circled Josiah and smiled, exposing tobacco brown teeth Mitch had never noticed before. She raised one foot over the bug and toed the remains into oblivion.

The hair bristled on Mitch's neck. "But, why are you…why were you so nice to us? You played games with us!"

Patty grinned. "Remember now, I taught you games to sharpen your wit and senses. You especially liked those games of quick reaction, didn't you?"

"Oh, my God!" Mitch said out loud.

"I never cared much for preacher talk." Patty stood, nimbly working three switches together into a braided stick, two flies hovering over the process. "And never could figure how the Lord would save a wretch from his own end."

"You played games with us so we would like you!"

"You understand me, boy." She continued to braid the switch, which ran down the length of her skirt.

"You lied to us," Mitch screamed. "You cheated!"

"Lying, well sure. But I never, ever cheat at my parlor games. You cheat at games and no one will play with you."

"You're a witch!"

Smirking, Patty swatted a fly to the ground and looked up from her handiwork. "You know, I prefer to be likened to a proper hostess, thank you. I keep a fine parlor. Don't you agree, boy?" She patted Josiah on the head. He didn't move, and she continued. "A hostess … she has power. Why, she knows where and when her guests sleep." Patty tied a knot at the end of the switch and chewed off the surplus stick, throwing her head back to laugh.

"You're the most evil person I ever met!"

"I suppose you might say that," she said. "Clever as I am. But hey, now that you're here, this place isn't that bad. You just might like your life with me. I can see you're a smart one…I can use one of those."

Mitch's clothes clung to his skin while newly arriving flies buzzed his ears and head. The meadow had taken on a dank, sewage-like smell. "Why do you want me? I want to go back home."

"Looky here, Mitchey-boy. Don't be scared. You have options. You be one of my gang boys and we have no trouble between us." Her black eyes sparkled like shiny buttons. "You try to run, and slave boy you'll be. Them … well, sometimes I keep them, sometimes I sell them." She paused. "And sometimes, I kill them for good."

Mitch noticed Josiah staring at him, and not into the woods. Gnats flitted in and out of the boy's moist eyes, but he didn't blink. Not once.

I have to fight.

Mitch yelled, "Why me? Why do you want me? I don't want to be a gang member!"

"You'll learn to like the ways," Patty whispered.

"I don't want to stay with you. You're a murderer!"

"You're good pickings." She didn't laugh this time and started to pace.

"But, why do you want me? I don't belong here!"

Patty eyed Mitch, raised her switch above her head, and sliced it down onto Josiah's frail back. The boy flew forward from the sitting position and lay face-down on the ground, groaning.

"So, you think I save my wrath for the colored ones? He's only my practice boy."

Mitch lurched to Josiah's side and pulled him up. "Josiah! I'm so sorry!"

A streak of maroon blood seeped through the shirt on Josiah's back. He hunched over his own knees and barely stood. But, to Mitch's surprise, he ably dashed a steady pace into the woods.

Patty didn't follow. "I told you, he's mine, boy. And now, you're next."

This time, Mitch ran. With his clothes sticking to his sweaty body, he ran as fast as he could. As he put distance between him and Patty Cannon, he could hear her laugh the laugh that had at one time made him happy. He glimpsed over his shoulder as he ran and saw her standing firm in the sunlight, rubbing the pistol in her belt.

Mitch crashed through the brambles and entered the dark woods, calling, "Josiah! Where are you?" His heart pounded against his chest but he didn't stop. He ran through the dancing shadows, vines and thicket, and over fallen, rotten logs.

"Josiah!" Mitch yelled, moving through the musty woods, his hands pushing off the cool bark of tree after tree.

Nothing.

"Josiah!" Mitch yelled louder, knowing Patty could hear his call and was probably following him.

BOOM. BOOM.

Mitch jolted to a stop and gulped in his next breath.

That was a gun. She shot the gun!

He leaned against a tree and whispered, "Josiah, please be here. Please be okay."

Nothing.

Mitch heard nothing except for the steady buzz of summer beetles.

Chapter 9
Wednesday Morning.

BOOM!

Mitch's eyes popped open to see his pile of *Cosmic Comic* books where he left them on the floor the night before.

"Where's Josiah?" he leaned against the beanbag chair. "Where's Patty?"

He stroked his rumpled hair, squeezed both of his own arms, and scanned his room. Nothing had changed. He stood and pulled up the window blinds to see the morning haze ooze over the lawn.

It's early.

He tiptoed to his bed and sat.

Did she kill Josiah?

Mitch hugged his crumpled pillow.

Why is she even coming after me?

Vroom.

The minivan engine softly rumbled from the driveway as Mitch's mom left for work. Still tiptoeing so he didn't wake Annie, he snuck downstairs in time to hear Fritzi barking from the neighbor's front steps. Mitch darted to the kitchen and found the newspaper sitting neatly on the table next to his mother's empty coffee cup. He sat and opened it full spread to the obituaries, the rooster clock ticking behind him.

Mitch frantically ran his finger down the "J" column looking for the name Josiah. "Josiah, Josiah, Josiah." Nothing.

He collapsed back on the bench and swept his hair off his forehead, grabbing it in his fists. "She's driving me crazy!" he said, dropping his hands in his lap and staring at the tabletop. "He must be alive…but, I don't even know if Josiah is real!" He got up from the table and sped to the den, where the fatigued *National Geographic* magazine remained on the leather chair.

"Who is Josiah?"

For the next hour, Mitch poured over the article, desperately circling and underlining words and phrases in pencil as he looked for clues. By the time Annie woke up and came downstairs, he had given up. Nothing in the article mentioned the infamous Patty Cannon keeping company with a boy named Josiah.

"Mom's gonna kill you when she sees you marked up that magazine," Annie teased as she sneaked around a corner.

Mitch slammed the magazine shut. "Don't do that to me!"

"Ooh. We're back to creepy, tense Mitch again, aren't we?"

He groaned. "I have a lot to do. Don't mess with me, okay?"

Annie squinted her eyes and glared at him. "What's wrong with you?"

"Ugh!" Mitch ran both hands down his face. "I'm just...tense. Okay? You're right, I'm tense." He looked up at his sister. "I'm tense about doing my summer essay. I have to get it done."

Annie stood in front of Mitch. "Well, pull it together. Since we don't have swim practice, you can spend your whole day at the library with me."

"Ah, come on." Mitch slumped back into the chair and put the *National Geographic* over his face. "You don't even like the library."

"Sure I do. I'm going to email Dad," Annie sang before she breezed out of the den and into the kitchen.

Mitch closed his eyes underneath the magazine.

DEAD: Anna Maria Burke, Pain-in-the-Butt Little Sister, Age 11

After breakfast, Mitch and Annie rode their bikes to the library and locked them to the side of the automatic front door.

To Mitch's relief, the Library Lady was not in and kind Mrs. Harris set him up with a computer terminal, per his request, in a quiet corner—away from Annie. He settled in to the most remote terminal available while Annie skipped to the carpeted periodicals room.

When he opened his email box to check for mail, Mitch found nothing but the theme details for the evening's swim meet:

To: Free_Style@aol.com

To all Ladybugs

Come prepared to swim for...
The Wild West!
Cowboy hats and boots are the style for tonight.
Yee-ha!

"No way," Mitch muttered. "They're not going to catch me wearing a cowboy hat with that swimsuit."

Click.

He deleted the email and sighed. "Nothing from Dad." Mitch rested his hands on his lap, rubbed his neck, and looked across the ancient, but pleasantly familiar library.

Annie was lying on her stomach on the floor of the periodicals room, her heels to her rump, flipping through five or six glossy teen magazines spread before her. Mrs. Harris read a romance novel at her desk, and a busy mother cruised the children's reading room with her four kids.

Maybe I'll email Dad later.

He closed his email box and logged on to the Internet.

He typed "PATTY CANNON" into the search engine and watched the computer screen roll down and stop after a few seconds.

Results 1-10 of about 28,000 for Patty Cannon.

PATTY CANNON house and tavern in Reliance, Delaware
PATTY CANNON Administers Justice, a book about her exploits…
PATTY CANNON ESTATES. A subdivision on the Delmarva Peninsula.

They built a subdivision named Patty Cannon Estates? Isn't that like naming a bunch of houses after Jack the Ripper?

He shook his head and turned his eyes back to the screen.

PIRATE PATTY CANNON and her son-in-law Joe Johnson ran a slave sale trade…

They really called her Pirate Patty?

PATTY CANNON The Monster's Handsome Face. Her gruesome story…

As Mitch read the site descriptions, sweat bubbled up on his palms. Each paragraph described the woman he had come to know in the meadow—tall, athletic, entertaining, and wicked. Not one site disputed the fact that Patty Cannon had been one of the most evil people to walk the east coast in the 19th century. But, none of the sites mentioned Josiah.

What if she shot him?

He sat back in his chair and exited the Internet. He stared at the computer terminal and decided to go back to his email box.

Hi Dad, how are you? I haven't heard from you, but I know you're busy.

Mitch hesitated a moment and then returned to his message.

I know I'm not supposed to tell you anything that will make you worry, but I'm having some weird dreams that are bugging me. They started off real cool, with a lady I liked, and now they're turning bad. Did you ever have weird dreams when you were my age?

See ya, Mitch

Mitch sent the email, closed his eyes, and sat back to think. The buzz of the fluorescent lights and the calm and quiet of the library overtook him and he soon fell asleep in his chair.

He opened his eyes in the middle of the woods. He was leaning against a thick-barked tree and panting as if he had just been running. He gasped when he realized he was back in Patty's woods and immediately thought of Josiah. "Josiah!" he called out.

"Mitchey-boy!" Patty's voice rose from somewhere on the other side of the thicket.

Mitch darted behind the tree trunk.

Ping!

He flashed his eyes open to the cool blue of the computer screen. Mitch sat up in his chair and shook his head hard. Never before had Patty come to him during a nap. His heart raced. He looked at the screen and saw that his father had replied to him.

He's there!

He punched open the incoming email.

I can't talk right now. You must find Josiah. He can help you.

Find Josiah?!

Mitch hurried an email back to his dad.

How do you know about Josiah????????

"Who's Josiah?" Annie whispered over Mitch's shoulder.

Chapter 10

Wednesday Evening. Swim Meet.

Mitch leapt from his chair and hid the blue screen with his back. "Go away, Annie!"

"I'm not going away. I came over here to email Dad." Annie stretched to peek around Mitch and at the flickering screen. "Who's Josiah?" She spoke in a loud, clear, booming voice. Mrs. Harris looked up from her paperback novel and put a finger to her lips, hushing the pair without making a sound herself.

Mitch strained to look over his shoulder while blocking the computer screen. He was able to click the window closed with his extended pinky finger. The email closed and the secrets he penned his dad fizzled from his sister's sight. "We have to go," he hissed.

Annie abandoned her line of inquiry and the two pedaled home in silence, and then on to the pool for the swim meet. Once on Ladybug territory, Annie and Mitch walked through the noisy locker rooms and to the pool deck, glancing up at the grassy ridge overlooking the competition. So far, Mrs. Burke had not arrived on Parents' Hill.

The triangular red and white meet flags flapped on ropes across the dazzling pool as the Clerk of Course, a stout and tanned veteran swim team mom, handed out stopwatches on neck cords to the volunteer timers. The smell of chlorine wafted through the scene and the younger Ladybugs chanted, "Fear the Bug! Fear the Bug!" Daryl, the Ladybug's coach, reviewed the team roster on his clip board. In keeping with the evening's Wild West theme, the tall blond coach confidently sported his lycra swim team suit, a faded straw cowboy hat, and Western boots. Mitch avoided him for as long as he could.

The drifting smell of burnt hot dogs from the grill on Parents' Hill signaled the impending start of the meet, sending stray Ladybugs wandering to the coaches' corner. Mitch shuffled around the pool deck, his towel strategically draped over his left shoulder and down his front. Annie followed, reciting instructions. "Okay. So, the plan is to ignore the coach and his cowboy get-up, and maybe he'll forget we missed practice."

"Sure." Mitch's mind was not on the missed practice.

The two approached their team corner, where Annie stooped to remove her red and black flip-flops. "Look!" She thrust her arm forward and pointed. "There's mom!"

Just as Mitch spied his mom on Parents' Hill, the Clerk of Course approached her. Mitch noticed the multiple stop watches hanging from the Clerk's neck.

"Annie, I don't know why you're so worried about getting in trouble. You never do."

"That's not true. Remember when Dad grounded me for a month in third grade? All's I did was start a club on the playground."

"You started a *nose picking* club. You had every kid on the playground picking their noses. For weeks!"

"I did that so anyone could join. No special skills required. The club didn't exclude anybody." Annie's eyes shifted back to Parents' Hill. Mrs. Burke nodded her head while she listened to the Clerk of Course, and then propped her bag and folded lawn chair down against a large shade tree.

"Mitch, look!" Annie jumped on her toes as she pointed to her mother. "She's coming this way."

Mrs. Burke teetered down the steep grass hill in her heels and walked, her slender arms swinging at her sides, to the opposite side of the pool deck. The Clerk of Course handed her a stopwatch, even though Mrs. Burke was clearly dressed for work and not poolside duty.

Annie squealed, "Mom's a volunteer timer!"

"Cool." Mitch waved at his mother across the pool.

Annie jumped on a white plastic stool. "She's going to be so busy concentrating on timing, she won't be able to talk to Daryl!"

"Yup." Mitch sat on the end of a lounge chair.

BUZZ.

The swim meet buzzer beckoned all swimmers to their team areas. Annie jumped off the stool and hustled to the huddle under the Ladybug's team umbrella, which consumed a corner near the deep end of the pool. Mitch took his time and wandered to the outside of the flock. Daryl coached the team on his Winning Plan, and then reminded them that ladybugs bring good luck—a concept that Mitch did not buy into. Then, he led them in the team chant.

"Fear the Bug! Fear the Bug!"

On the other side of the pool, near the shallow end, the Woolly Mammoths growled and grunted, pumping arms and pounding chests from atop lounge chairs and tables.

Why can't our team be called the Sharks?

Daryl distributed swim cards for the events and heats and each swimmer joined his or her assigned group. Since there were so many 11- and 12-year-old girls on the team, Annie would only be swimming two events—freestyle and breaststroke. Because there were so few 13- and 14-year-old boys, Mitch would be laboring through several events against the Mammoths—free, breast, backstroke, butterfly, and the dreaded individual medley.

He took his cards and sat with the other boys in his group, clutching the towel to his chest and chewing on his synthetic goggle straps.

Boys, 13 to 14, 100 Meter Freestyle.

Mitch's first event was called and the boys manned their positions on the side of the pool, towering over each lane. He was not the best freestyler on his team, but not the worst either. The six lanky competitors—three Ladybugs and three Mammoths—curled their toes over the pool ledge, hunched their backs over their feet, and waited for the buzzer to blast. Mitch stared into the crystal clear water of the pool, his eyes on the black stripe waving on the bottom of his lane. Hot dogs still burned on the grill.

BOOM!

A gun?

He heard a gun instead of a buzzer. Conflicting images roared through Mitch's head, but he dove into the pool and began to swim anyway.

He could see through the froth and waves that the other boys were swimming and people were cheering them on. No one had stopped. He plowed ahead faster, swimming over the shadows of the currents swaying on the pool bottom, and touched the rough plaster of the first wall before any of the other boys. He flipped underwater, pushed off the wall with his feet, and set off for the next length of the race.

As he swam, Mitch heard his dad's voice, "Find Josiah." He swam faster.

Mitch tagged the next white wall underwater and flip-turned. When he rotated his chin out of the water to breathe, he saw Josiah's face looking down at him. "Find Josiah," his dad's voice said again. Mitch was terrified and didn't know what to do besides swim.

How does Dad know Josiah?

He swam. He swam faster. And faster. In one huge lunge he grabbed the smooth rim of the last wall several feet before his closest opponent, choking back a flood of chlorinated water. His, now barefoot, mother jumped up and down on deck at the end of his lane and hugged his soaking wet frame as he pulled himself out of the water.

"Mitchell, you did it! You took your first freestyle first!" Pool water sparkled on her face and on her arms, and the front of her linen skirt absorbed enough water to turn it an entire shade darker.

Mitch bent over at the waist with his hands on his knees to recover. His chest heaved and his shoulders hurt.

"Mom," he finally captured his breath. "Do you or Dad know somebody named Josiah?"

Chapter 11

Wednesday Evening. Josiah.

In spite of the distractions, Mitch swam the best meet of his life, propelling himself to two first places and three seconds. Never before had he beaten a Mammoth. And, never before had he ribboned in all of his events.

On the ride home, Mitch and Annie each leaned out their windows and listened to the evening's harmony of starlings and bullfrogs bounce off the moving car. Mitch stargazed and tried to follow one particular bright star, which alluded him in the black sky.

There are so many, it's hard to focus on one.

By the time the three of them made the quiet ride home and rolled into the dark house, they were ready for bed and mumbled goodnight to each other at the bottom of the stairs. Even Mitch, who was terrified to fall asleep, faithfully brushed his teeth and tumbled into his narrow bed. He propped up his tired body, with his back to his headboard, and his pillow folded against his stomach.

Dear God, why is all this happening to me?

Cosmic Comic number 54 sat on the top of the bedside stack. As he stared at its illustrated cover, Mitch's head nodded forward twice before he fell asleep.

He woke, still clutching the tree in Patty Cannon's woods. The heat of the late afternoon rested on the treetops, like a lid on a shoebox.

Find Josiah.

His father's words rattled his conscience. Mitch took a deep breath, pushed off from the rough trunk, and stumbled over the underbrush of sticks, logs, and tangled ferns that paved the way before him.

Which way should I go?

Footsteps crunched in the leaves behind him, forcing Mitch into a frenzied run. He ran further into the trees—which were tall and dense, like stage curtains—and away from proper daylight. The steps continued to crunch somewhere far behind him.

Are they real, or my imagination?

He stopped and wiped his face with his muslin sleeve.

What's real and what's my imagination anyway?

His heart fluttered and he continued on. The leaves on the ground grew mustier, darker, wetter, and more compact as he forged deeper into the woods. Creek water gurgled nearby.

"Psst! Psst!"

Mitch stopped and listened. Slowly, he turned in the direction of the noise.

Please don't let it be her.

"Psst! Mitchey, it's me." A boy's voice came from below. Mitch bent over. "Josiah, is that you?"

"Shh! Don't talk none. She's comin'." A skinny finger waved at Mitch from under a large fallen tree. Its rotted roots and trunk rested in the ravine below Mitch and the broad leafy top on the bank across the creek. "Quick now."

Mitch followed the brown finger. He sat on the steep hill and slid down to the tree on his butt. Damp leaves and cool mud oozed up his backside and into his pant legs. He landed by the tree at the bottom of the ravine and rolled on his side, under its base, to join Josiah.

In the mud of the creek bank, Josiah had dug what looked to be a bear den out from under the tree. Once Mitch rolled inside, Josiah scurried to cover his entrance with sticks and muddy, mossy brush. Both boys fit in the space, although it was taller than it was long. To sit, Mitch pulled his knees to his chest and bent his head forward. Josiah sat cross-legged before him.

"Josiah, what are you doing here?"

"Mitchey, I come here to help ya. Ya gots to go." Josiah looked straight into Mitch's eyes with the same message of urgency he had delivered in the meadow. "She's gonna kill ya."

"What about my dad? How do you know my dad?"

"Mitchey, I said she's gonna kill ya."

"I'll get her first! Better yet, I'll just stop dreaming about her." His chin bobbed on his knees.

"It don't work that way, no it don't." Josiah spoke slowly. "This ain't a dream, Mitchey. And, on the missus's turf, she kill, she don't ever git killed."

"Not a dream? You mean, this is for real?"

Josiah nodded his head. "Ya gots to go."

"What about my dad?"

Josiah shifted on his rump. "I ain't seen yer pappy fer a long time."

"But you know him!"

"Ya gots to go." Josiah glanced toward the door he had configured from the brush.

"Why can't I just wish her out of my dreams, and change everything?"

"It don't work that way. She done got ya on her turf, in her time. The only way outta the mess is to escape from here. I seen that, Mitchey."

"How do we do that?" Mitch asked.

"*We* don't do nothin'. Ya gots to do it by yerself."

"You have to come with me!"

"Shh!" Josiah frowned. "She'll be hearin' ya."

Mitch lowered his voice, "Why can't you help me? I thought we were friends."

"I kin help. I jes' cain't go with ya."

"Why not?"

Josiah leaned into Mitch. "She gots me, Mitchey. She gots me when I was awake. What ya see is kinda like my spirit self. I'm stuck in her territory."

"You mean you're dead?"

Josiah settled back, "Dead'n your world, stuck in this one."

This time, Mitch leaned forward, "You mean, like purgatory?"

"Don't know what that be, but it don't sound nice." He peeked out the opening.

"How do you know my dad?" Mitch tried to see through the brush as well, but his hands trembled when he moved a support stick, so he stopped.

Josiah moved the brush back. "Look, ya don't have much time. She's real good at playin' hide 'n seek. Jes' know that I helped yer pappy once, a long time ago."

"Helped him do what?"

"Ya gots to go!"

"What do you mean 'go'? Where am I supposed to go?"

"Ya go north. Way to the free north where'n she and her gang cain't git you. Ye'll be free if ya can git north."

"I'm having a hard time understanding this," Mitch said, rubbing his chin between his knees. "Why is she coming after me?"

Josiah brought two fingers to his lips. "Shh." The boys sat in silence, listening for noises that never came, until Josiah carefully removed the barrier to the cramped den. When he finished he said, "Come," and climbed out of the hiding place. Mitch followed.

On his hands and knees, Josiah led Mitch down the sloppy bank, stopping at a mound of mud alongside a bend in the creek. He stood and pointed to the mound, again putting his fingers to his lips. Then, he knelt down over the heap and dug with both hands. Disturbed earthworms crawled for their lives as he dug and dug until he found what he was looking for—two ghost-white bones. One long and smooth with balls on either end, and the other flat, yet curved.

Josiah stood tall by Mitch and raised the bones in the air. "This fella asked too many questions and didn't go when I told him to."

The bones hung before Mitch's nose, their crusty tips and smooth curves screaming to be touched. Mitch kept his hands at his sides. "But, those could be...could be deer bones." He thought back to Annie. "Like the ones my sister found!"

"They ain't, Mitch. They ain't."

The two boys stood quietly until Josiah knelt back down to respectfully rebury the bones. Suddenly, Josiah jumped up from the mound. "Mitchey, she's comin'!"

"What?" Mitch froze in the mud.

Patty Cannon's voice floated through the curtain of trees. "Mitchey boy! Come along. I'll let you shoot the gun."

Josiah grabbed Mitch by the shoulders. "Ya jes' gots to go!"

Chapter 12
Thursday Morning. Power Failure.

BOOM!

Mitch woke to the sound of a gun. His eyes scanned his dark room and settled on the glowing clock on his bed stand. It read, "5:15 A.M."

BOOM!

He jolted up in bed and listened.

Is it her? Is she following me?

A flash of white light blasted through his blinds and thunder rumbled outside.

BOOM!

"Thunder," he sighed and slumped back in his pillows. Rain pelted the windows. He lay on his side and thought of his Italian-American mom who prayed for everything.

Dear God, please make Patty Cannon go away.

BOOM!

Mitch turned back to the clock. The bright yellow numbers now screamed, "5:19 A.M."

He slipped on shorts and a T-shirt, left his room, and snuck downstairs, tiptoeing to the mudroom door. He opened it so it wouldn't creek and stood on the side porch, sheltered from the downpour.

"Fritzi better not bark," he mumbled.

Mrs. Burke complained that no matter how early she woke up, the neighbors woke up earlier and tossed their annoying dog outside. Rain or shine. Once the little tyrant woke up the neighborhood, they retracted him into the quiet of their home.

From the porch, Mitch jumped into the grey, driving rain and ran to the newspaper lying in a plastic bag on the driveway. He bounded back to the house with as few leaps as possible.

Fritzi barked as Mitch neared the door. "Shoot!" He entered the house, slowly closing the door behind him. "Stupid, dog. You know I'm the only neighbor who likes you!"

DEAD: Fritzi, Cute But Annoying Dachshund, Age 2

Mitch dried off with the kitchen towel hanging from the refrigerator door handle. He heard the yaps of the dog, and the neighbor loudly hushing him and bringing him inside. The automatic coffee pot on the counter beeped that a fresh pot was ready.

Gotta hurry before Mom wakes up.

He pulled the newspaper out of the wet plastic bag and laid it on the table, dropping the bag on the floor. Standing, Mitch flipped through the local Metro section and stopped at the obituaries. He sat down and inhaled deeply.

"Allen, Alrami," Mitch ran his finger down the alphabetical column and stopped at the B's. "Baley, Bremmer, Burke, Busch." He stopped, then backtracked. "Burke?!" He hunched over the paper and looked again.

Alfred Burke, Jr.

Mitch relaxed in his chair.

Duh.

His dad's name was Thomas, not Alfred. And Alfred was black, not white like his dad.

"Good morning, swimmer star," Mitch's mom leaned over his shoulder and kissed his wet cheek. He sprung out of his chair and crumbled the paper to his front.

"Mom! Why did you sneak up on me like that?"

"Good morning to you, too." She poured a cup of coffee. "Where do you think this rain is coming from? It was such a beautiful night last night—not a cloud in the sky. No swim practice in this weather." She picked the plastic bag off the floor, put it in the sink, and sat.

Before Mrs. Burke left for work, she interrogated Mitch on his summer essay. The progress he reported was acceptable to her, so she left happy, and oblivious. By the time Annie came down the stairs at eight o'clock, Mitch had decided he needed her help. When she stocking-slid into the kitchen, he was waiting for her at the table.

"Whoa!" Annie said as she looked at her brother. "You look awful! Did you even go to bed last night?" She peeled a banana and ate it as she stood at the sink.

"Look Annie, I think I need your help."

"Really?" Annie slid to the table and plopped down in a chair. "My big bro needs his little sister's assistance?" Chewed banana oozed between her teeth when she grinned.

"I have a secret to tell you. You have to promise you won't tell anyone."

Annie stiffened in her chair. "The last time you told me a secret, I knew it already." She tilted her head. "Actually, I was the one who told it to you. That's how lame your secret was."

Mitch leaned forward and whispered. "This one's about Patty."

Annie's blue eyes widened, pushing her eyebrows up to the fringe of her crown. "Are you going to tell me who Josiah is?"

Mitch loudly exhaled, his fists clenched on the table. "That's just it. He comes with Patty Cannon."

"He's not a school friend of yours?"

Mitch shook his head.

"Wait a second. So, how does Dad know about Josiah?"

"I don't know! Mom said she never heard of him." As best he could, Mitch rattled through his summer dreams with Patty and how once he had welcomed her and now was afraid of her. He told her everything. Everything that is, that he knew.

"Are you sure you don't need a shrink instead of me?" Annie stood from the table, crossed the room to the refrigerator, and opened the door.

"I knew I shouldn't have opened my mouth to you."

"Okay. Okay." She peeked around the door of the refrigerator. "I'll be nice."

Mitch stood. "I need to talk to Dad. Or email him. Now."

Annie didn't question her brother and instead hastily changed clothes and followed him outside to the bikes. Although the rain had stopped completely, the bike path was clear of other riders and they quickly pedaled the two miles to the library, where Mitch hopped off his bike, dropped it at the front door, and yanked off his helmet. A hand-written sign was taped to the door:

CLOSED: POWER FAILURE DUE TO STORM

Mitch threw his helmet on the grass and fell on the lawn.

"This means you can't email Dad, right?" Annie stayed on her bike, her feet on the ground.

Sitting, Mitch hung his sweaty head in his hands. "Now what? What do I do?"

Annie got off her bike and propped it upright against the library door. She sat next to Mitch and put her arm around his shoulder. "Big bro, you need to get rid of this lady. I think she's driving you nuts." She scratched her nose. "You have got to pull it together."

Sweat trickled into Mitch's eyes. "I'm trying. I'm even praying to get rid of her." He rested his chin on his knees. "And I've been praying to God that Dad is okay and comes back to us. I don't know what else to do."

"Well, first of all, you're praying all wrong." She removed her arm and dusted wet grass off his shoulder. "If you think Dad is gone and you want him back, you have to pray to Saint Anthony, not God. Mom always prays to Saint Anthony when she wants things back. He's the patron saint of lost things, or something like that."

Mitch drew his eyebrows into a knot.

"It's easy, just say, 'Dear Saint Anthony, please bring my dad back to me.'"

Mitch did not smile and kept his eyes on his sister.

"Second of all, you do know what to do." Annie rose. "You've got to run. Just like Josiah said." She pointed north. "You've got to escape to Canada, like the fugitive slaves in the history books."

"What?"

"I read your *National Geographic* article."

Mitch stared at his blond little sister, standing with her hands on her hips.

Josiah and Annie are right.

Beep! Beep, beep!

"Oh, no! It's Mom!" Mitch jumped up as his mother's car pulled into the steamy, empty parking lot. "Act normal," he said and wiped his face.

"Hey, you two." Mrs. Burke said from the van window.

Annie walked to the car while Mitch picked up his bike. "What are you doing here, Mrs. Burke? Shouldn't you be at work?"

Their mom giggled and said, "I decided I'd stop in and have lunch with you. I'm dropping off my books on the way." Mitch stood with his bike and watched the interaction.

"And," she continued. "I received a wonderful email from Dad, who has a message for my anxious son." She winked at Annie.

"You did?" Mitch smiled for the first time that day. "What did he say?"

Chapter 13
Thursday Evening. A Way Out.

The email from Mitch's dad actually didn't say much and, it certainly didn't mention Patty Cannon, or Josiah. But Mitch was satisfied.

His unit will be moving again. And he's really hot and he's really hungry for a steak. And, he'll call me later.

Mitch tossed that happy thought over and over in his head as he sat on the stool at the kitchen counter. He smiled to himself.

I think he'll be okay.

Mrs. Burke decided to take the rest of the day off from work and stay home with her kids. Thunder rumbled again while she and Annie embarked on a cookie-making expedition. In the commotion of flying flour and chocolate chips, Mitch snuck off to the den, where he laid the *National Geographic* article out on the floor.

I have to find a way out.

He flipped through the article he had already read, scouring the pages for clues and details. He wouldn't be able to communicate with his Dad today, and sleep would definitely come at nightfall. He needed to figure out—and fast—how he was going to escape from Patty.

A map? Could there be an escape map? A map, maybe, that led slaves to Canada?

Mitch concentrated on the spread in front of him. Nothing in the magazine article, however, pointed to a map. He analyzed every word of every paragraph and every face of every photograph. More than once, he turned to Harriet Tubman's own solemn, mesmerizing face.

I wonder if she can help.

Mitch lay back on the floor, his head resting on a tan velvet pillow he took from the couch. His eyes scanned the room and finally rested on the floor-to-ceiling bookshelf his father had built. Each shelf was neatly lined with his dad's hardcovers. Hemingway, T.S. Elliot, Mark Twain, Steinbeck… Mitch inspected the classics on the middle shelves and then scoured the top shelves, where he read the titles embossed on big, fat books—*North American History*, *U.S. History*, *The History of the Americas in the 19th Century*.

Dad sure loves history.

Mitch read on—*The History of Maryland, The History of the Eastern Shore, Remembering Slavery, The Monster's Handsome Face.*

"Hmm?"

He rose from the floor and approached the bookcase. Standing on his tiptoes, he pulled a thick black book off the shelf by its spine and turned it over in the palm of his hand.

The Monster's Handsome Face: Patty Cannon in Fiction and Fact

Mitch's hands trembled.

I saw this title on my Internet search.

He could barely hold the book as he sat down in the leather chair, his index finger on the picture of a glowing white human skull on the front cover.

Mitch slowly opened *The Monster's Handsome Face* and delved into the old text. Page after page was underlined in pencil, and then in pen. Blue, then faded red. Mitch read on about Pirate Patty. She was wicked by anyone's description, and was known to burn wriggling slave babies alive when they fussed. After she was captured, Patty poisoned herself in the Georgetown, Delaware, jail while waiting to be hanged by the court. All of this information was underlined in bright red ink.

"Dad knows her, too," he whispered. "That's why he sent me to Josiah. He knows them both."

He tucked the book back in its place on the shelf and fell back in the leather chair, stunned.

Now what?

He closed his eyes.

I can't tell Annie about this. It's too weird.

"Dinner, Mitchell!" His mom called from the kitchen.

Mitch, his mom, and Annie ate at the dining room table, usually reserved for Sunday meals and special occasions. Rain dropped outside, but the thunder and lightning had stopped. While Annie and her mom told family stories by lasagna and candlelight, Mitch pretended to be interested and listened quietly. But, his thoughts were firmly planted on the escape he had to make that evening.

I'll get Harriet Tubman. Harriet Tubman will help me.

After dinner and a distracting game of Scrabble, Mitch excused himself and went to bed. Before getting under his sheets, he washed his face and brushed his teeth until the toothpaste ran dry in his mouth. "No telling when I'll be able to do this again," he mumbled.

He climbed into bed, followed his routine of pulling the clean sheet to his chin, and listened to the television drone softly downstairs. Mitch took several deep breaths and waited for sleep to come, but the drowsy wave failed to overtake him.

Creeeeak.

His bedroom door opened.

"Annie, what are you doing in here?" He was startled and relieved at the same time.

Carrying a small canvas tote, Annie crept into his room and sat on the foot of Mitch's bed. "Shh, don't let Mom hear." She turned the tote upside down on the bed.

"Look, I brought you some supplies for your trip." The tote gaped open and out fell a flashlight, a compass, a tube of sunscreen, a pocket camera, and a plastic bag of peanuts … the kind with the peanut-man dancing along the top.

"You thought of everything." Mitch picked up the greasy sunscreen tube and chuckled. "But, how am I supposed to carry this stuff in my dreams?"

"Don't be such a dork." She lined up the travel items in front of her brother on his bed and arranged her fingers in a teepee. "Focus. Just look at these things and memorize them. Then hopefully, you'll find them in your dreams."

"What?!"

"Don't you ever read those magazine articles that tell you how to control your dreams?"

"Can't say that I do."

Annie sighed. "Focus really hard on something before you go to sleep and it will enter your subconscious. Then, you'll dream about it."

"Do you really think I'll need sunscreen and a camera?"

Annie hesitated and then reached for the tube. "You're right. Your skin doesn't burn, so you won't need the sunscreen. But keep the camera so you can show me pictures." She removed the sunscreen and pushed the camera closer to Mitch.

I give up.

"Thanks, sis."

Contented, Annie turned to go, leaving her brother to prepare for his journey. But, Mitch wasn't entirely ready.

"Hey, I think I have a plan."

"You do?" Annie leapt back to the foot of the bed. "What is it?"

Mitch whispered, "I read that Patty Cannon lived about 20 miles east of Harriet Tubman. You know who she is, don't you?"

"Lord, Mitch, do you think I'm stupid?" She wedged her hands into her hips.

"You're using the Lord's name in vain."

"I am not."

"Anyway, I'm going to find Harriet Tubman in Bucktown, Maryland and ask for her help."

"Wow, do you think that'll work?"

"It's worth a shot. She helped tons of other people escape."

"Yeah, well. They were all black slaves from plantations. You're a white boy from Clean Drinking, Maryland."

"It's worth a shot."

"I guess." Annie dropped her hands from her hips and stood by his bedside, staring at him.

"Okay, you've got to go now." Mitch fluffed his pillow.

"I'll see you in the morning." Annie snuck out of the room and gently closed the door.

Mitch moved Annie's items off the bed. "I hope so," he muttered and lay down on his back, his face to the plaster ceiling.

Chapter 14
Thursday Night. Ready, Set, Go.

Mitch woke up in the woods, face down in Josiah's mound of freshly packed mud.

"Quick! Crawl back under the tree!" Josiah yanked him forward by the back of his shirt collar and pushed him up the bank. "Git!"

Mitch wiped the cold mud from his eyes and scrambled along the creek bank, to the familiar fallen tree. There, he shimmied on his belly like a lizard and back into the safety of the hidden den under the tree. Josiah slid in behind him and hurriedly filled the den opening with downed pine branches, leaving a hole just large enough to peek through.

"Mitchey, Boy! Did I hear you in the woods?" Patty's voice rang in the distance, clearly echoing after each spoken word. "Josiah! Come out, boy!"

The two boys breathed heavy as they worked their bodies deeper and deeper into the mud den. Josiah stole a breath and whispered, "Go now! Go down through the creek so she and the gang cain't track you." He paused. "She's right east of us. You go west and I'll head her off to the east."

"I'm not going until you tell me about my dad."

"Ya gots to go!"

"Tell me about my father." In spite of the leaves and mud, Mitch managed to cross his arms over his chest.

Josiah lunged over the inches between them and clutched Mitch's muddy shirt. "So be it. Yer pappy was here. She had him a long time ago." Sweat poured from his delicate face. "I helped yer pappy git away," he blurted.

Mitch pulled Josiah's rough hands from his shirt and held them in his own. "Why? Why did she come for him … and now me?" He stared nose to nose with Josiah. "And why did you help him, and now me?"

BOOM!

A gunshot cracked in the distance.

Josiah, his fists cupped in Mitch's, pounded Mitch's chest. "Jes' go!"

Mitch tightened his grip on the fists. "Tell me, or I stay with you."

BOOM!

Josiah dropped his sweaty chin to his chest. "Alright." He met Mitch's eyes.

"Yer great-great-great-great-grandpappy, Lawrence Burke, turned the missus's pappy in for murder. He saw the missus's pappy—he was called Lucius Hanley—shoot another man dead, and he done git the sheriff."

"No way." Mitch released Josiah's fists.

"Yessir. And the sheriff and his men done gone and kilt the missus' pappy, that Mr. Hanley Sir. They done hung him like a ham in the town square when the missus was only a chil' of thirteen or so. She stood lookin' on." Josiah shook his head. "The missus never done forgive yer Grandpappy Lawrence."

The smell of mud and rotten tree clung to Mitch's nostril hairs. He wiped his nose and rested his own hands on his knees. "And, she's trying to get revenge on all of us. On my family?"

Josiah nodded his head and turned to the peephole he had created. "She done want to kill off yer family name."

"Jeez."

"Now, I told ya the lot." Josiah peered back through the pine branches.

"Wait a minute," Mitch touched Josiah's bony shoulder. "What about you? Why are you here?"

Josiah shut his lips tight, his eyes still on the den's peep hole.

BOOM!

Another gunshot blast through the woods, but it was no closer to the hideout than the other.

"Josiah, I'm not budging until you tell."

Josiah looked at his bare feet, then at his hands, then at Mitch. "I'm the missus' slave boy."

"Slave boy? That's not right…"

"She owns me outright, Mitchey."

"But…it's not right. Run with me. We can escape together."

"I cain't. My feet are done stuck here, in this world. Now ya gots to make sure she don't do the same to you."

"But, there's got to be a way to get you out. At least, out of this place."

"There ain't."

"There's got to be." Mitch shook his head to organize its clutter, but nothing fell into place. "Josiah, I promise you I'll figure out a way."

Josiah peeked back out through the brush. "Well, that sounds fine, but ya gots to go."

"Okay, okay. I'll go. But first, tell me how to get to Bucktown, Maryland."

"Are ya touched in the head?" The slave boy released a pine branch, letting it brush against his own bewildered face. His words rattled from his mouth. "Bucktown be down south. Ya wanna be goin' north. The gang will be findin' ya in the south. That's her territory, Mitchey. Her stompin' grounds."

"But, Bucktown is where Harriet Tubman lives. I need to find her so she can help me escape on the Underground Railroad."

Josiah scrunched his face, still buried in the branches. "What are ya sayin'? Who's this Harriet lady?" He leaned further forward to peek out the peephole again. "And, I don't right know what this Underground Railroad thing is."

"Please. Just tell me how to get to Bucktown, and I'll find Harriet Tubman."

With the art of having said it before, Josiah explained that the best way south was to first get on the Nanticoke River and ride it as far as possible. There was a boatman at the river's far edge named Wilson Lee who helped runaways and would help Mitch. "Ya git into his shed and hoot like an owl." Josiah cupped his hands to his mouth and softly hooted, "Hoo, Hoo. He'll come find ya when he's ready."

"Hoot," Mitch practiced under his breath. "Wilson Lee, I have to remember, Wilson Lee."

"Be careful who ya take help from. Some of the peoples are good, and some are as evil as the missus."

"How do I know who's good and who's not?"

"Ya'll learn the signs." Josiah put his finger to Mitch's knee. "Ya think back to the parlor games that the missus done teach ya. Keep yer wits sharp-like and stay in top form." Josiah spoke slowly, allowing his words special emphasis. "Ya gots to be in top form."

Mitch and Josiah sat in silence, listening for hints of Patty, until Josiah spoke. "On the count of three now, ya go west and I'll run her off at the east. You'll run about a mile's pace before ya come to the river. Drop south and turn the bend to the boatman's place. Go right to the old shed and wait. Wilson Lee'll git ya on the river goin' south. Git."

In an instant, Josiah crashed through the brush of the den and ran back towards Patty's meadow. Mitch hesitated and then ran in the opposite direction.

Dear God, help me.

Mud to his ankles, he sped downhill, over the mound that covered the bones, through the shallow creek and to the opposite bank. Soon, he heard screaming in the direction of Josiah's run to the east.

She found him!

He turned to the west and ran like he never had before.

Dear God, please help us both.

Chapter 15
Mitch Meets Wilson Lee.

For what seemed like hours, Mitch could think of nothing but running. He ran through the sweltering heat, out of the woods, and onto the open meadow Josiah had told him about. This meadow, unlike Patty's, seemed to never end. He stopped and focused on the heavy golden sun setting low before him.

That's west. Good, I'm where I'm supposed to be. The river should be south of here.

He swatted the blood-sucking mosquitoes from his ears and face and drew in long breaths, recapturing his strength. Mitch cautiously glanced over each shoulder and half-stood, hunching to stay hidden in the tall grass. He tracked the setting orb and kept it to his right.

What if someone sees me?

He hunched even lower and ran.

Crickets and bullfrogs volleyed chirps back and forth as dusk settled on the meadow. Josiah had promised him that the hike to the river from the meadow would not be a far one, and it wasn't. Within fifteen minutes, Mitch reached the banks of the Nanticoke River.

"Wow."

The dark, wide, and flat river rested under the rising moon, not a ripple or current breaking its stillness. Downriver, a large flat-bottomed canoe, filled with empty burlap sacks, was tied to a craggy pier's pilings and floated gently against them. On the banks, barely visible above the pier, stood a small wooden shed that was no bigger than his father's den.

That's gotta be it.

Mitch sloshed along the bank in the wet reeds and stopped when he came to the shed. The sky turned from light grey to dark grey, and was making its way to black. Without knocking, he opened the door and stepped inside, where true dark had settled.

I hope Josiah is right.

Mitch's eyes soon adjusted to the dark and he found himself in the company of paddles, white buoys and strings, and long poles hanging from the interior walls. The musty interior smelled of wet rope and dried fish.

The owl. Remember to hoot like an owl.

"Hoot, hoot," Mitch called through his cupped hands. He waited and heard nothing but the bullfrogs.

"Hoot, hoot." He tried again.

Nothing but bullfrogs.

"Hoot, hoot."

Creak.

Mitch jumped backward into the darkest corner, knocking a tattered fishing net on a long pole off the wall. The shed door opened and an imposing man stooped through the doorway and entered the shed with a hearty step. His white skin and grey bristle beard glowed under the light of the lantern he carried. His eyes, Mitch noticed, were the same blue color as the water at the Ladybug swimming pool. He didn't smile, but he didn't frown either and Mitch kept quiet.

"Hoot yerself, boy." The man faced him. "I done hear ya the first time ya called. I've been 'spectin' ya. Josiah sent word days ago."

Mitch relaxed his shoulders, but stayed in the corner. "Are you Mr. Lee?"

"Nope." The tall man set the lantern on a short shelf and sat on a dirty pickle barrel. "I'm Wilson Lee." He wiped his brow with his shirtsleeve. "Ya can call me Wilson, or ya can call me Lee." He paused. "Or, ya can call me Wilson Lee. Together like that. Jes' don't call me Mr. Lee."

"Yes, sir."

"An don't call me sir, neither." Wilson Lee craned his stubbled neck to get a closer look at Mitch. "Why, boy, yer high yeller."

"Excuse me, sir? I mean Wilson. I mean Lee."

Wilson Lee smiled a broad grin.

"I mean, Wilson Lee. What's high yeller?"

"What's high yeller? Why boy, you've got white blood in ya." Wilson Lee leaned toward Mitch and squinted his chlorine blue eyes. "Yep, yer skin is dark and light altogether like. Jes' like them high yellers I've seen from down south."

Mitch shifted against the shed wall. "Well actually, sir. I mean Wilson Lee. I am white. I'm part Italian. That's where I get my dark skin. From my mother's side."

"Really, now." Wilson Lee sat back on the barrel. "Never heard of no Italians this corner of the ocean."

Mitch stepped away from the wall. "Sir, um Wilson Lee. Could you get me to Bucktown? Josiah thought you could."

The boatman rubbed his chin and stood up, towering over the runaway.

"Son, I know ya got that pirate woman on yer tail. It'd be a might better idea to get you north and outta this neck of the woods." He lowered his voice. "Ya know she knows this place like the back of her grimy hand. Her family runs a ferryboat jes' a spat from here."

"I really think I need to find Harriet Tubman and she lives in Bucktown." Mitch paused. "She can get me north. She knows the way."

Wilson Lee put a weathered hand on Mitch's shoulder. "I don't know any one by that name, but if ya insist, I can git ya on yer way. We'll go down river to Vienna and spend the night." He turned to the door. "I'll find ya a way to Bucktown from there."

"Thank you, Wilson Lee."

"Jes' follow me, don't talk less ya have to, and do as I say. As ya go forward, jes' always keep yer mouth shut about where ya been and who done brought ya."

"Yes, sir. Wilson Lee."

The boatman retrieved his lantern from the shelf and led Mitch out of the shack, through the reeds and to his canoe, which majestically awaited its evening cargo. Stars flickered in the night sky as he nimbly ambled into the craft and motioned for Mitch to follow. Mitch sat next to the glowing lantern while Wilson Lee readied his long paddles and unhooked the thick pier lines. He took the seat next to Mitch and pointed to the heap of stained burlap sacks. Next, he spoke in a hushed whisper, "Ya need to get under them bags so as nobody sees ya." He pointed again.

"Oh." Mitch scurried to the bottom of the wobbling boat and to the pile. He buried himself on his back under the burlap until he couldn't see a thing and waited for Wilson Lee to finish covering him up. The bags were damp and reeked of fish, Mitch's least-favorite food.

Gnarled wood ate into Mitch's spine as he lay on the floor, and the smell of fish enveloped his face, but he didn't complain. The boatman pushed the canoe from the pier and set it on a course downriver. "Next stop, Vienna, Maryland."

The subtle swell of the river pushed the rugged boat forward. The frogs croaked their passage and the night birds swooped above them in the moonlight. The boat ride was smooth and the swish of the paddle hitting the flat water soothed Mitch's nerves.

"Steal away, steal away." Wilson Lee softly sang. "Steal away to Jesus." Mitch listened to each soft, gentle word as it hung in the still sky, and then fell asleep under the weight of the rough, moldy, burlap, which shrouded him, for the time being, in safety.

Chapter 16

Mitch Meets Mary.

A hand grabbed Mitch's shoulder and shook it.

"Mom?" he mumbled.

He opened his eyes in the darkness and ran his fingers along his covers. Instead of smooth, cotton sheets, he felt the rough weave of the burlap.

What? I'm still here?

He peeked out from under the burlap pile.

"Boy." It was Wilson Lee. "Boy, we jes' got a bit of time before we get to my sister's place. Follow me and keep low." In a swoop, he pulled a sack off of Mitch.

Why haven't I woken up?

Mitch's racing heart screeched to a halt. A moment passed before it thumped awake. He removed the remaining burlap and followed Wilson Lee out of the teetering boat. The boatman secured the paddles and tied the boat to a single wood piling on the riverbank as Mitch stood on the banks and rubbed scratchy burlap threads from his arms.

I should be awake. I should be in my own room.

He shook his head to wake himself up.

Why am I still here?

The night sky was black as uncooked coal, but the bright stars lit up the shoreline like twinkling spotlights. Mitch didn't hear the frogs or birds here, but he could see a small village nestled inland from the river. Wilson Lee had trudged up the steep bank and was waiting for Mitch on a dirt ridge. He held the lantern high until Mitch reached his side. "We go straight away to Mary's cottage. She'll feed ya simple and then put ya to bed. If yer lucky, I can git ya on a carriage in the morning."

Mitch nodded and followed Wilson Lee along the edge of a foggy open field to a small white cottage that stood alone, a candle burning on its porch. The boatman motioned for Mitch to hide behind a berry bush beside the back wall, while he addressed the house.

"Hoot, hoot," Wilson Lee called.

Sure sounds like an owl when he does it!

The door of the cottage creaked open and Wilson Lee motioned for Mitch to come. The two took one step up and entered into the sliver of light. The smell of hot cornbread and clean floors pulled Mitch easily through the entry. A woman held the door open and closed it quickly behind him, peering into the dark outside beyond Mitch's shoulder as she did so. Mary was a tall woman, like her brother, but her features were finer. Her skin was paler and her grey hair was wrapped in a bun atop her head.

"Patty Cannon's men are here, brother," she said in a low voice. They've come to town jes' this night."

Mitch stood paralyzed by the door while Wilson Lee crossed the small room and sat at a sturdy wooden table, his lantern parked in the middle.

"They looking for the boy?"

"I'm supposing. I hear they told the tavern keeper they're 'on a hunt.'" Mary rubbed her veined hands together and focused on her brother, not Mitch, who remained at her side. "We should get him out in the morning, when that Johnson gang will be nursing whiskey headaches."

Wilson Lee nodded from the table and motioned Mitch to join him. "Johnson is the name of Pirate Patty's thieving son-in-law. She done put him in charge of her evil-doing gang."

Mitch sat across from Wilson Lee. "Yes sir, I mean Wilson Lee, I know."

Mary crossed to the table herself and removed an iron pan of the enticing cornbread from a basket there. She served her brother and Mitch the bread, whipped butter, and dried fish.

Mitch's stomach turned at the thought of eating the pungent fish, but he was hungry, and didn't know when he would eat next. He swallowed unchewed chunks down with swigs of thick milk, trying to douse the strong fishy taste with the dairy. Both Mary and Wilson Lee left the crumb-topped table. When they returned, Mary placed a small linen bag in front of Mitch.

"In the morning, ya'll be leaving early. Take these biscuits for the way. Don't talk to nobody about who kept ya, and stay outta the way of people in general." Mitch listened intently and Mary continued. "Ya'll be taken by carriage toward Bucktown. It'll be a long day, so rest when ya can." Her chest rose and then lowered as she captured her breath. "My brother tells me ya insist on meeting up with this Tubman woman. Is she expecting ya?"

"No, ma'am." Mitch reconsidered and looked directly into her crystal blue eyes. "I don't know, ma'am."

"No need to call me ma'am." Mary folded her hands in front of her cotton muslin skirt. "Where's her home sit?"

Mitch shifted in his chair. "She's a slave woman, ma'am. I mean, Mary. I think she lives on a large plantation."

"A plantation, ya say? Why, she must live on the Brodess place. That would be the only large farm in Bucktown." She wiped her hands on her skirt. "It's not rightfully a plantation, mind ya, being as they don't have so many slaves. But, it is a sizeable farm."

Mitch had nothing to say, as none of this made sense to him. He just wanted to find Harriet Tubman. Mary gently took his chin in her hands. "Ya jes' make sure she's kind, ya hear?"

He nodded.

"And not like that Patty Cannon creature you're running from. Now git to bed." Mary led Mitch to a corner of the cottage where Wilson Lee had laid down to sleep. She showed him the coarse blanket and pillow she had placed under her brother's bed. "Squeeze under there and I'll pull them covers down aside ya. Jes' in case anybody stops to visit."

Mitch obeyed and squeezed into his sleeping space. Mary pulled the hand-stitched quilt off her brother and neatly covered the side of the bed with it, hiding Mitch behind it. Then she left him, crossed the room to latch the front door, and snuffed out Wilson Lee's lantern.

The hardwood floor was not as uncomfortable as the boat bottom had been, and the space was surprisingly free of dust and cobwebs, but Mitch still couldn't sleep.

What if Annie is right and Harriet Tubman doesn't help white boys?

His thoughts squeezed his heavy head.

What if Patty knows where I am?

The smell of cornbread, and the boatman's loud, steady snore filled the small cottage. Mitch stared at the cracked bed slats above him. The dusty straw mattress that held Wilson Lee sagged between the slats and almost touched his belly.

Dear God, please don't let it break.

Chapter 17

The Rosses.

"Brother, they're here!" Mary shrieked.

Mitch could hear Mary crossing the room to Wilson Lee's bed. The man's snores came to an abrupt halt.

"It's the Johnson boys, I hear their ruckus!" Mary spat the words out of her mouth. "And tomorrow has yet to come!"

What do I do?

Mitch curled into himself behind the quilt hanging down from Wilson Lee's bed, but moved the overhang just enough to the side so he could peek into the room.

Without the luxury of properly waking, Wilson Lee sat up, leapt to the cottage door, unlatched the lock, and stepped outside. Mary flew about the cottage. She moved swiftly and quietly, loading a shotgun she had brought out from around her fireplace.

Mitch rolled to his belly and out from beneath the sagging mattress and abandoned bed.

Creak.

Wilson Lee stepped back through the front door. "Sister," he put his hand up when he saw she carried a gun, "It ain't the Johnsons. The ruckus you hear is the boy's ride. Murphy saw the Johnson gang on the other side of town and thought it best to leave now, afore they take their drunken control of the streets." He turned to Mitch. "Git the bag Mary done packed ya and come along." Mitch did as he was told and snatched the small but heavy sack of Maryland beaten biscuits from the table.

Wilson Lee held the door while Mary gave Mitch a quick hug. Mitch tumbled out the door into the night and, with a helping hand from Wilson Lee, directly into the rear of a wooden wagon led by a robust black horse. The driver sat up high above the wagon load with his back to his cargo. As he had done on Wilson Lee's boat, Mitch hid on the floor. This time, he was covered by a fabric tarp, topped with chunks and pieces of dirt the size of placemats. Wilson Lee told him the squares were "peat," and not dirt. He also told Mitch not to talk to the driver.

"Murphy don't want to lay eyes on or talk to anyone he helps escape. That way, he kin honestly tell authorities that he 'didn't see no one or talk to a soul' when they go and ask him about runaways. Stay quiet and he'll git you to that Brodess place you're wanting to go to."

Talk with Murphy would've been difficult anyway. Wilson Lee had created an ample breathing space for Mitch, and he was hidden under only one layer of peat, but his surroundings weren't suited to conversation. The musty smell of the peat moss seeped into Mitch's pores and his nose. He tucked the bag of biscuits in his shirt, wrapped his arms around himself, and closed his eyes to avoid the falling dirt flecks from the peat. The wagon jostled over road pits and bumps and swayed back and forth, but the horse at the helm kept a steady pace. Mitch could feel the beast's power as the wagon moved on.

Dear God, please help me find Harriet Tubman.

Mitch thought back to what Annie had told him.

"Mom always prays to Saint Anthony when she wants things back."

But does that work if you never had the thing in the first place?

He distracted himself with this thought until he fell asleep.

Hours later, with the first hint of morning, Mitch woke to the sound of Murphy, hooting like an owl in his seat.

"Hoot, hoot."

Why am I still here?

Mitch carefully moved a piece of the peat and raised his head just enough to get a look at the back of the hooting driver. Murphy's reddish hair was cropped close, exposing a wide neck—the sign of a patient and sturdy man. With the reins in one hand, he pointed down the road with the other. "There she is, boy. That's the Brodess place."

A large, but not huge, white house stood a few hundred yards from the wagon. "The slave house is to this side, closer to the fields."

Mitch squinted through the murky morning to see an unpainted shack that sat astride a cornfield. The entire house looked lopsided to him.

"Ya need to crawl out the back of the wagon by yerself and head for the slave house. They'll be preparin' for the day before that master wakes and puts 'em to work. They'll take care of ya." Murphy took hold of the reins with both hands. "Git."

Mitch threw the tarp from his body, patted his shirt to make sure Mary's bag of biscuits was still there, crawled on his knees, and out the back of the wagon. As soon as his feet hit the hard dirt of the road, Murphy moved the wagon forward.

I'm on my own.

Mitch ran off the road, through the dewey cornfield and towards the shack. As he approached the front door he could see the glow of a woodfire burning inside. He slowed to a walk and caught his breath. He heard whispers and what sounded like a baby cooing. Softly, he knocked on the door and waited.

What should I say? How should I act?

One of his dad's lectures jumped into his mind.

As a man, always be the first to introduce yourself when you meet new people.

The shack door slowly opened and a tall, muscular, shirtless black man peered out. A woman holding a baby in one arm and a lit candle in the other looked over his shoulder.

That must be her.

Mitch looked right around the man and to the woman. "Good evening, I mean good morning, ma'am. My name is Mitchell Burke." He stuck his right hand out towards the woman and watched his own arm, from his shoulder to his fingers, shake slightly.

"Who the hell are ya, boy?" The man barked the question, forcing a deep wrinkle into his brow.

Mitch pulled his shaky hand back to his side. "I'm sorry, sir. I'm Mitchell Burke and I came to meet Harriet Tubman. I mean, I need her help and I guessed she could get me to Canada. Patty Cannon is after me and wants to make me her slave, or kill me, or both, and I don't know how to get out except for Mrs. Tubman's help. Sir."

The man yanked Mitch by his shirt into the shack and closed the door behind him. "Son, ya look a right mess. Are ya sane, boy?"

"Yes, sir." Mitch tugged at his own shirtsleeve with his opposite hand. "I just need to speak with your wife, sir. I really need her help."

The woman with the baby in her arms and the imposing man looked quizzically at each other. The woman was clearly pregnant and four or five other small children slept in the corners and crannies of the shack. The smell of hard work and frying pork filled the tight space.

The man spoke slowly. "Why is it ya be needin' my wife, boy?" His words were firm, but not threatening. "That Cannon woman is an evil witch. What kin my wife do 'bout her?"

Mitch swallowed. "Sir, Mr. Tubman. I need your wife to tell me how to get out of here. How to get to safety."

Again, the couple looked at each other and the baby wiggled in her mother's arms until she slithered to the floor. The father spoke. "I ain't no Mr. Tubman, and this ain't no Mrs. Tubman, boy. Why, I'm Ross, Ben Ross.

And this here is my wife, Rit Greene. Now, Harriet is her given name, but she ain't no Tubman."

The child on the floor squealed at her father and he picked her up. She squirmed until he put her back on the floor. This time, she crawled toward Mitch, who was concentrating on Ben Ross' words. His eyes swelled with tears.

No Harriet Tubman?

"Are you sure? Harriet Tubman is supposed to be here. On the Brodess plantation!"

The mother stepped toward Mitch and rested her hand on his shoulder. She was a petite woman with soft skin and a milk and honey voice. "Now hear ya, son. Don't be worryin' none. We'll git ya some good salt pork and corn fritters and ya kin rest awhile here." She picked the baby back up. "Ben's not here every day, ya know. So we done made a good breakfast afore he has to git up an' go."

Mitch didn't hear her words. "How am I going to get away from her?" he blurted.

"Wa!" The baby cried out in Rit's arms and one of the other children stirred on the floor, but didn't wake up. Ben Ross stepped forward.

"Boy, no Tubman woman lives 'round here. But, we kin help. Ya don't need no Tubman woman to git ya on yer way."

"But, you believe me, don't you? That I'm being chased by Patty Cannon?"

"Nothin' not to believe, boy. She's done chased every kind and every color." Ben stopped and thought for a minute. "How'd ya git this far, son? That witch lives a ways of here."

"Josiah told me…"

Never tell who brought you or who helped you.

"I had help, sir."

Ben Ross nodded and pulled his shirt from a rusted nail on the wall. He slid it over his head and tucked it into his britches and turned to Rit. "We'll be eatin' and goin' afore long." Rit handed the baby to Ben and stepped to the fireplace to turn the pork in the sizzling iron skillet.

Mitch stood, helpless. "Where will we go?" He asked as the man gathered belongings and put them in a sack, doing so with the baby tucked into the crook of his left arm. Mitch surveyed the shack and the sleeping children.

They're all so little.

"You can't leave your family, Mr. Ross. I mean, your kids must need you."

Ben sat to eat Rit's meal, resting the baby on his knee. "Mitch, ya said yer name was?" He grabbed a chunk of greasy pork with his fingers. "I'll be happy to share my meal with ya before we leave."

"But, your family…"

"Boy, I leave my family every day. I don't live none here." He pushed the pork into his mouth and continued talking. "'Nother master owns me. Ten or so miles west of here. It's a special occasion that brings me here in the middle of the week." He bounced his knee. "Araminta here is startin' to walk at last, and Rit and I decided we gone to sneak a visit to celebrate." The baby squealed again, her teeny teeth peeking out of her pink gums.

"You mean, you *sneak* here?"

"Now, only on occasion. Usual like, the master allows a visit ever so often."

Rit appeared at Ben's side. "Ya need to git afore the houses wake." She took the squirming baby from Ben's knee and handed him a cloth sack. The baby, sparkling drool on her chin, pointed to the front door.

Mitch remembered the sack from Mary in his baggy shirt and patted it to make sure it was still there. Ben rose and said, "My horse is in the woods. We'll take her to the Transquakin' and I'll git you on a raft up towards the Choptank."

"The Transquaking, sir?" Mitch knew by now to add the "ing."

"A quiet river…not too many eyes on it."

BOOM.

"It's the master!" Rit, with the baby on her hip, blew out the candle on the table.

What?

Ben moved fast and pushed Mitch out the door of the shack. "Run to them woods! Master Greene must be awake."

Mitch stumbled outside the door in the haziness, but Ben Ross' strong hands pulled him up.

BOOM.

"Keep yer head down low and run between the corn." Ben Ross led the way.

"What's happening?" Mitch whispered. Mature corn stalks slapped him in the face as he followed the father.

"Don't know, boy. Jes'run."

BOOM. BOOM.

Ben Ross ran like a spooked deer from the cornfield and into the woods.

Mitch trailed far behind. "Mr. Ross!" He finally penetrated the dense woods but didn't see Ben Ross, or the horse. "Mr. Ross. I can't see you!"

BOOM.

"Mr. Ross! I think it's her. I think it's Patty Cannon!" Mitch stood by himself under a dark, imposing, pine tree. "Please come out."

Dear God, please let me wake up in my own bed.

Chapter 18

Friday. Early Morning.

BOOM!

The bedroom door swung open and hit the wall.

Mitch's prone body buckled in bed. "What's happening? Where are you?"

Annie blew into the room carrying the handset of the telephone. "Here I am!" She jumped onto Mitch's bed, her pajama bottoms rolled to her knees, and shoved the silver receiver into his startled face, giving him no time to argue with her. "Sleepy head! It's Dad!" She leaned into his ear. "Dad is on the phone for you!"

"What?" Mitch took the cordless phone and put it to his chest, instead of his ear. "I'm awake?"

"Answer the phone! Dad's in a line using a satellite phone. He doesn't have all day!" She bounced off the bed and landed on the floor. "Say, 'Hello, Dad!'"

Mitch rubbed his eyes and put the phone to his ear. "Dad?"

"Mitchell, it's me, Dad. Listen, I don't have much time. Get Annie out of the room."

The voice of Mr. Burke had a caffeine-like effect on Mitch. His mental fog lifted and he sat up straight on the edge of his bed. "Annie, leave my room and shut the door behind you."

"What do you mean, 'Leave my room?' You never say 'please.'"

"Annie, go! Dad doesn't have much time!" Mitch threw a pillow at her.

"Okay, okay. But, I'm taking these with me." She snatched two *Cosmic Comic* books from the nightstand, skated out of the room, and slammed the door behind her.

Mitch opened his mouth to protest, but instead jerked the phone to his ear. "Dad, Dad? Are you okay?"

"Listen up, Mitch. I'm fine. Our unit is moving again and I wanted to get through to you before we lose communication. Mitchell, you've got to run from Patty Cannon. Don't let her keep you."

"Dad, I know. I know a lot. I talked to Josiah. He told me everything."

"Everything? Is he still okay? Is Josiah okay?"

"I think so."

Jeez. I hope so.

"Dad, I'm running." Mitch spoke confidently. "And, I've read some of the stuff in your library. I'm trying to find Harriet Tubman so she can get me north, but I think Patty is chasing me."

Static rattled the line.

"Harriet Tubman? Mitchell, listen. Tubman wasn't born until 1822. Patty Cannon lived on the Eastern Shore until 1829. Harriet Tubman is either not born yet, or is just a child. She can't help you."

What?

"Do you hear me, Mitch? Are you there?"

"I'm here, Dad."

Harriet Tubman can't help me?

"Then how am I supposed to get out?" His voice cracked. "I was counting on Harriet Tubman. She saved all of those people…"

"Look, you can do it. I did and I know you can too. You have to keep your wits about you and think. Don't panic. Think every move through, Mitch. Do you understand?"

"Yeah. Okay, Dad."

"Mitchell. I can't do this for you. You have to use your wits to beat Patty at her own game. That's the only way out. And Mitch, you cannot let Annie or your mother know about Patty."

"But Dad, Annie already knows. I told her."

"Does she know why Patty is coming after you?"

Static crackled again, giving Mitch the time he needed to think. "Do you mean because I'm the great-whatever grandson of someone who turned her murderer father in to the authorities?"

"Yes."

"Well, no. I never told her that part."

"Don't."

"Why not?"

"It'll scare Annie and get her worrying. Patty Cannon preys on people who are at their most vulnerable. And, don't tell her that Patty came after me as well. Don't put Annie in that position. Let's just worry about you."

"Vulnerable?"

Dad was vulnerable.

"When have you ever been vulnerable, Dad?"

"Patty Cannon came to me about thirteen years ago."

"Why then?"

"Mitchell, I've got to hang up." Mitch could hear his father tell another man that he was hanging up. His turn was over.

"Dad, do you have to hang up now?"

"Gotta go, son. Tell mom I called to say "hi," I'll call again, and nothing else. Don't tell her anything about Patty Cannon. Got that?"

"Dad?"

"Yes, Mitchell."

"I'm scared."

"You have every right to be. But, you can do this, son. I love you."

Click.

The phone connection died and Mitch flopped backwards on the bed. His head throbbed. "What am I going to do now?"

Creak.

The bedroom door opened—softly this time. Annie peeked in the room and entered when she saw Mitch was off the phone. She was now dressed in her red and black swim team suit and ladybug flip-flops and was still holding onto Mitch's comic books. Mitch stayed on the bed. "Go ahead. Ask me. I know you're dying to know what Dad said."

Annie hopped onto the bottom of the bed and sat up on her knees. "Well, I have a surprise for you, Mr. Smarty Pants." She smacked Mitch's stomach with one of his comic books. "I don't care what Dad said to you. I had my own private conversation with him. I want to know what happened with Patty Cannon!" She sat back on her behind and dangled her legs over the edge of the bed.

Mitch sat up. "Where's Mom?"

"Work, where do you think? You slept *way* late. She told me to let you sleep until swim team … but man, you're cutting it close."

"Annie, do you remember Dad thirteen years ago?"

"You are so lame. I wasn't even born thirteen years ago."

Mitch slouched. "Ugh, right." He rolled his fingers around the corner of his quilt. "Harriet Tubman can't help me. I got all the way to Bucktown, and she wasn't there."

"But, you got to Bucktown without getting caught?"

Mitch nodded.

"Cool. Did you use my supplies?"

"Your supplies?"

"Yes, my supplies. Don't you remember? Flashlight, compass, camera, and bag of peanuts." Annie ticked the list off her fingertips. "Did you?"

Mitch stood and rubbed his face. "Um, no."

She frowned.

"Well, I must not have needed them. Maybe they would've appeared if I had needed them."

Annie stood and faced Mitch. "Maybe I shouldn't have bothered."

"Come on, Annie. I have a headache. Don't make it worse."

"Fine." Annie walked to the door, chin out, holding her head high. "I'll meet you downstairs. The coach is coming any minute to drive us to swim team. Mom arranged it." She exited the room with the comic books crunched against her chest.

"What?" Mitch called after his sister.

No answer.

"Annie!" he yelled. "Can't we ride our bikes?"

Chapter 19

Friday Morning. Swim Team.

Mitch didn't speak in Daryl's car until they arrived at the pool. "Please drop me off here," he said as they passed the front metal gate.

Daryl was everything but the picture of a *ladybug* coach. He was tall, blond, cut out of rock, and handsome in a "geeky" sort of way, as Annie would say. Swim team rumor had it that he attended college on a swim scholarship and swam more than he studied.

"But, swim team enters the back gate." Daryl looked in his rear view mirror at Mitch, sitting in the back seat.

"He wants to look at the newspaper at the front desk." Annie popped up. "You know, get his obituary fix for the day. He didn't have time at home."

"Could you just leave me alone?"

Daryl stopped the car. "Hey, I think obituaries are cool. I've been reading them since my grandma died."

"Why would you do that?" Annie asked. "They're creepy." She opened the car door and swung her legs out the side.

"You actually learn a lot about character from them. Like, how people don't lie." Daryl winked at Annie. "And maybe, how people keep commitments. Like swim practice."

Mitch sprang out of the car. "I'll meet you on deck."

The morning was hot and steamy and a haze blanketed the sky. He walked barefoot and shirtless through the gate and to the front desk. Tony, the desk attendant, smiled over his morning soda. "Morning, dude." He slurped from the cold can and slid the *Metro* section of the newspaper across the desk to Mitch. The *Style* section stayed with Tony.

Mitch tossed his towel over one shoulder, bent over the newspaper, and turned to the obituary page. He scanned the page from "A," stopping abruptly at "P."

Pipman, Roger. Sgt. Roger Pipman was killed in Iraq in an attack on an Army logistics operation in Baghdad. Pipman leaves a wife and a young baby. He re-enlisted in the Illinois National Guard in the hope of finishing a 20-year commitment to the Guard.

"God. Another one."

By the time Mitch arrived poolside, Annie was swimming warm-up laps with the team. He avoided Daryl and his teammates, tugged at his skin-tight trunks to lower them on his legs, dropped his towel, and dove into the choppy water of lane five, where the frigid water enveloped him. He free-styled through his first 100 meters and then switched to breaststroke, welcoming the shift on his muscles. His headache disappeared as he swam meter after meter, concentrating on his thoughts instead of his strokes.

What am I going to do without Harriet Tubman? Dad thinks I can handle this.

The coach's whistle blew, but Mitch didn't hear it and swam on.

Maybe I can get back to Josiah.

He swam.

But, he said he couldn't leave Patty's place and I had to go on by myself.

The whistle blew again.

What if Ben Ross leaves me in the woods?

He swam faster.

I'll never get out of there.

The whistle blew and his teammates yelled from the deck.

What if Ben Ross helps me, gets caught, and never sees his family again? That baby girl wouldn't have her dad.

Mitch could barely hear the yelling from the deck.

What about Dad? Why did she pick on Dad? I can't ask Mom. He told me not to.

"Lame brain!" Annie screamed from the deck.

Why me?

"Mitch. You're supposed to stop swimming!"

Mitch touched the wall and noticed green polished toes wrapped over the edge of his lane. He surfaced to Annie standing before him with the entire team huddling behind her.

DEAD: Mitchell Thomas Burke, Idiot, Age 13

"Go, go, go, go!" the entire Ladybug team mocked at lane five.

Mitch stayed in the pool and hung quietly on the wall. "Yeah. Thanks alot, Annie."

She left and the coach's long toes took her place at the lane. "Give me 400 more meters, Burke. You pick the stroke."

"Eight more laps?!" Mitch was exhausted.

Daryl nodded and turned to the team. "Ladybugs," his bare chest lifted as he bellowed. "Relay time!" He blew the whistle and within seconds, the pool water churned like the white crests in the Chesapeake Bay, and Mitch began his own 400 meter sentence.

At the end of practice, Annie left the kids in her age group and wandered, her goggles still suctioned to her face, over to her brother. He stood alone at the pool edge, shaking his legs and strategically wiping himself dry with the towel, so neither underarm hair nor lycra'd private parts were exposed to the general viewing audience.

"You were thinking about her, weren't you?"

Mitch draped the towel over his shoulders and down his front. "I was not. What makes you think that?" he snapped.

Annie peered into his face. "Because she drives you crazy."

"Duh." He tiptoed barefoot over the prickles in the grass. "I've got to figure out how to get north." He made his way to a lounge chair under a shade tree and sat.

"If you would listen to me, I could help you." Annie followed and stood by the lounge. "You need a plan."

Mitch laid back on the lounge. "Easy for you to say. You're not being chased by a killer."

"I'm serious. Remember Coach Daryl's Winning Plan: Dream, which I think you've got covered; Plan; Work; and then Persist. You can't start working at your escape until you have a plan."

"I had a plan, remember? I was going to get Harriet Tubman to help me. Only, she's not born yet!"

Annie ignored his comment as she surveyed the pool area. The rest of the aquatic Ladybugs were oblivious to her brother's pain. "We'll start at the library this afternoon."

Before Mitch could spit out his protest, she waved and ran down the hill to her friend, Meghan. He threw his head back in exasperation and closed his eyes.

A plan. Right.

The hot sun fused with his 1,000-meter exhaustion and a sleepy swell immediately overtook him.

"Boy!" A voice called out.

Mitch jerked his eyes open in time to see Annie and Meghan jump into the pool together.

Don't go to sleep! Not now.

Mitch tried to keep his eyes open, but the late morning heat rested on his lids and drew them shut. They shut, eyelash by eyelash, and he fell asleep.

"Boy!" The voice loomed closer.

Chapter 20

Meeting Big Mo.

"Boy! Can ya hear me?" Ben Ross' hushed voice snuck from behind a neighboring tree.

"I'm here." Mitch repelled from the pine tree in the dull moonlight. "Here I am."

"Shush, ya! Git back by that tree and listen to me."

Mitch backed up against the moist pine, running his fingers over the mossy bark. The smell of decaying tree needles rose from the ground and blended with the pre-dawn fog.

"The horse is tied a bit from here. Ya best follow me now on my tail and we'll ride her to the river. Big Mo will be waitin' fer ya at the Best Pitch boat ramp."

Ben Ross didn't wait for a response, but bolted from his tree and into the darkest thicket of the woods. Mitch pushed off from the pine and followed as closely as he could.

BOOM!

"I think it's her, Mr. Ross. I think it's Patty Cannon!" Mitch spouted the words as he stumbled through the woods behind Ben Ross, who slowed down and looked over his shoulder.

"Don't matter who it is, boy. No friend o'mine shoots a rifle afore the sun come up." He approached a waiting horse, which was tethered between two trees, and hurriedly untied the worn leather straps, all the while stroking the animal's withers. Muscles from both owner and animal rippled and twitched.

Puffing, Mitch approached the pair. "Mr. Ross, what year is it?"

Ben Ross pulled himself up on the horse's back and extended a wide palm to Mitch. "Lordy, boy. Ya sure yer not touched in the head a bit?"

Mitch took his hand and struggled, but succeeded in mounting the jet black animal. As soon as he settled on the rough wool blanket on its hindquarters, the horse threw its head, turned, and set on a trail that only it could see. Mitch leaned into Ben Ross's sweaty back, but wouldn't let go of his question. "I just want to know what year it is." The horse walked, but didn't run, through the still woods.

"The year is 18 and 23," Ben Ross whispered. "We be in the month of August, in the year of 1823. That much I know."

The horse continued without any direction from its owner.

"1823?"

Dad said Harriet Tubman was born in 1822. She would be one year old now.

Mitch tightly held on to Ben Ross, but his thoughts rushed back to the Ross' family shack on the Brodess plantation and the baby girl pointing to the door.

That was her!

"You're Harriet Tubman's father. Your baby girl is Harriet Tubman!"

Ben Ross loudly clicked his tongue and shook his head. "Son, I know ya have lots to worry on, with that Cannon woman an' all. But, I'm gonna be glad to get ya on with Big Mo an' onto the river. Yer tirin' me some." He wiped his brow, causing Mitch to slip to the flank of the horse. "That chil' of mine's named Araminta Ross. Not Harriet and not Tubman."

Araminta Ross is going to grow up to be Harriet Tubman.

Mitch adjusted his position behind Ben Ross and kept his mouth shut until the horse left the woods and passed into an open meadow. The moon cast a steady light over their path as they neared a foggy marsh and a river. First came the co-mingled smell of tidal mud and wild reeds, then the clean smell of the fresh river water that was lapping the banks.

"Are we safe?" Mitch asked.

"If Big Mo is ready, yer as safe as ya'll be till ya get to freedom." Ben Ross swung one leg over the quiet horse and dismounted into the mud. He nodded to Mitch to do the same and he did, slowly sliding off the blanket, over the horse's bulging belly and to the ground, careful not to step on or be stepped on by the horse's hooves. Ben Ross dropped the horse's reins, patted its rump, and walked to the river. The independent horse stayed, but Mitch followed. They approached the river's edge where a wooden boat sat nestled in the marsh. Made of cut logs, it resembled a fat canoe with sail, running a good 25 feet long and ten feet wide. A compartment protruded from the deck, but existed mostly below and to the boat's center. Further forward, a small and lonely candle burned from the bow of the canoe.

Ben Ross turned to Mitch. "I see Big Mo is ready. Ya'll go with him up the Transquakin'. He'll get ya as far as a boat can go. From there, ya need to look for the other logger men that'll get ya into Cambridge and up the Choptank River. Take yer cues from the helpin' folk along the way. The rivermen knows the way the best." Ben Ross patted Mitch firmly on his back and jogged back to his waiting horse, before Mitch could say thank you or goodbye.

There goes Harriet Tubman's dad.

Mitch faced the boat by himself. It was much longer than Wilson Lee's canoe, and wider too. He slid down the grassy riverbank on his rear and landed at the side of the boat that was tied to a log piling, which rose four feet out of the marsh. "Hello?" he called from the shore. "Hello?"

A huge man sprang from the bottom of the boat. "Who's that?" His harsh voice landed in a whisper. He placed a massive hand on the boat's rimmed side and held a shotgun in the other. His shoulders rolled like the withers of the horse and the whites of his eyes, illuminated by the candlelight, glowed like toasting marshmallows against his black skin.

Mitch trembled at the sight and sound of Big Mo. He wanted to run, but knew he was stuck, there in the mud, alongside Big Mo's canoe. "Ben Ross brought me. He told me you would take me up the Transquaking River."

Big Mo released a huge bark of a laugh that bit the still air. "Ha!" He leaned over the side of the boat. "So, I'm supposed to take me another nigger boy up the river, am I?"

Nigger? He shouldn't use that word.

Mitch stuttered, "Uh, sir. I'm a white boy."

"Ha! Even more unlikely. Me haulin' a white boy!" He brought the barrel of his gun to his bulky chest and aimed down at his visitor.

Mitch splashed thigh-deep into the marsh and behind the piling for protection. The thick vertical log hid his thin frame from Big Mo's gun sights. "Go away!" he screamed.

"Yer gonna need more nerve than that, white boy. If'n ya wants to git outta here with me."

"I don't, I don't want to go with you!"

"Ya might be changin' yer mind when ya hears the ghost Lizzie Beth callin' after ya in the marsh!"

The boy clung tighter to the wet wood piling.

"Yep. Ye'll be callin' fer me as soon as she gets her headless body near ya."

"There's no ghost here!"

Big Mo's voice rumbled from the boat. "Most of us niggers, and fer that matter, all of the runaways, know that LizzieBeth lives right over there in that swamp." His sausage-like finger pointed to the other side of the river, where the reeds danced in the dark. "Ever since her massa cut off her head and tossed it in the swamp with her body … we all be knowin' she lives here now." Big Mo leaned on the butt of his gun. "She sings songs and howls at ya when ya travel alone."

Mitch's heart pounded all the way to his head. He searched the foggy swamp for signs of a ghost. The reeds continued to sway and an occasional frog croaked, but other than that, he saw nothing but the dark before the dawn. He did, however, feel a gentle breeze wrap around his neck.

"An' it's a shame. All she did were to steal some tobacco leaves fer herself. Jes' one or two." Big Mo raised two fingers. "An the massa cut off her head with the same knife LizzieBeth used to cut the bush. Tsk. Tsk."

Mitch inched from around the piling, up the bank, and closer to the boat. "How do I know you're not going to hurt me?"

"Ya don't none." Big Mo untied the boat from the pilings and began preparations to embark on the river. "How do I know yer not some spy, lookin' to turn in runaway nigger-lovers?"

"Don't say that word." Mitch looked at the sweaty, ill-tempered man and then down at his own swollen feet, sludge and reeds gushing between his toes. "I mean, you don't, sir."

"Then get in and down below. Done make no sound 'til I tell ya."

"Yes, sir." Mitch climbed aboard and into the hole under the plank hatch Big Mo had opened for him. The hatch clamped and he sank into a musky compartment that stored mildewed ropes, kerosene in barrels, and the occasional dead fish. Big Mo thumped above on deck as the boat loosened from the piling and moved onto the river. Mitch's stomach rumbled. Sitting in total darkness, he rustled through his shirt and removed Mary's bag of Maryland biscuits from around his side. He hurriedly ate one, not minding the dry crumbs sticking to the inside of his throat. A skinny mouse scurried from under a sack and sniffed at the crumbs that dropped from Mitch's shirt to the floor.

Mice!

Mitch kicked at the creature, sending it scurrying back the way it came. Careful not to attract more mice, he wiped the remaining crumbs from his body and curled into a ball, protecting himself from the rodent. He closed his eyes and concentrated on the sounds and rhythms of Big Mo on the deck. The huge man maneuvered the sail and the mast and softly hummed to himself as he worked. His melodic tunes danced with the creaking noise the boat made as it moved.

Terribly tired, Mitch finally had the opportunity to sleep, and he did, his head resting awkwardly on an oily, stout kerosene barrel. He slept soundly, not moving for hours until a haunting and eerie voice penetrated the morning air.

"Kneeeeeeeeeee bone in the mornin'."

The singing invaded the quiet and woke Mitch. He lifted his head from the barrel and strained to hear the haunting words.

"Ah, knee bone. Knee bone, didn't I tell you?" The words whirled like cigarette smoke through the boat's floorboards.

It's LizzieBeth!

"O Lord, knee bone bend."

Mitch sat up and scrambled behind the other barrels in the cramped space. Most of the barrels stood upright, but one or two laid on their sides.

Dear God, don't let LizzieBeth get me.

The boat hemmed and hawed and Mitch realized it wasn't moving and was docked again. Light poured down through the cracks in the hatch and voices other than LizzieBeth's rose louder and louder. Sweat swelled underneath his clothes.

"We trusts you got the boy, Big Moses!" A man shouted from the riverbank.

Big Mo's footsteps crossed above him and stopped directly over the hatch to Mitch's compartment. "Kneebone, didn't I call you? O Lord, knee bone bend." Big Mo sang before pausing to answer the men. "Don't know what yer talking 'bout fellas," he bellowed.

It's Big Mo, not LizzieBeth!

Mitch strained to hear the men on shore talk.

"Come now, Big Mo. One of the missus's boys done run and we heard ya mights got him."

It's Patty's gang! They found me!

Mitch's heart pulsated through his sweaty shirt. He could hear Big Mo pulling and dragging ropes on deck.

Where can I go?

"No niggers on this boat 'ceptin' for me." Big Mo moved about the deck and sang, "Knee bone, didn't I call you? O Lord, *knee bone bend.*" He laid special emphasis on these last words.

What is he saying? What is knee bone bend supposed to mean?

Mitch sat in the cramped space and rubbed his own knees.

What am I supposed to do?

The voices of the men grew louder. "We can see yer boat's not carryin' no cargo. No reason fer ya to be so high up the river with an empty boat."

Moses spoke, "Sees ya knows nothing 'bout the timber business here, Mr. Johnson. I load the boat with lumber in the yards over at Linkwood an' sail 'em downriver south to the Bestpitch point. I never come up the river with no logs, only on goin' down."

"The boy we speak of passes for white, Moses. We know he done run this way. Heard he's on to Cambridge."

Big Mo sang, "Oh, knee bone, knee bone. O Lord, knee bone *bend*." He thumped his heavy foot on the deck.

Another of the men shouted to the boat. "Look here. We got a notice an' it says the missus will give a reward for the boy."

"Knee bone, kneel, knee bone. O Lord, knee bone bend."

Knee bone bend. Kneel?

Mitch leaned forward, put his hand on a barrel for balance, and folded his legs under him in the tight space.

Should I be kneeling?

He leaned against the barrel to adjust himself, and it wobbled.

The barrel's empty!

"We needs to come aboard, Moses, else the missus would be thinking we didn't do our job."

"I don't got nothin' to hide." Big Mo walked back on top of the hatch and sang. "O Lord, knee bone bend."

That's it. I can't stand in the barrel, but I can kneel in it!

Mitch scooted to the base of the barrel, gently tilted it against another barrel, and crawled inside. Awkwardly, he knelt with his knees fused together and pulled the barrel back over himself, miraculously without knocking any of the other barrels over.

"We'll be comin' aboard then."

Mitch froze inside his barrel haven. Footsteps and verbal threats of at least three men swished and shot through the tall grass of the shore. He knelt, with barely an inch of space to spare, inside the dusty wooden barrel, as Patty Cannon's men approached Big Mo's boat.

Chapter 21

Leaving Big Mo.

Mitch struggled to hold the rim of the barrel to the floor with his sore fingertips.

Moses' heavy feet paced the deck, stopping when his voice thundered, "I's been a free man ever since my Pappy done bought my freedom. I's a free man on my own boat. You don't scare me none, Joe Johnson!"

"Make way, Moses. We don't want no trouble with ya."

The boat swayed as the men laid their hands on its hardwood side. Mitch heard the mass of Big Mo's body lunge across the deck, creating his own wind as he moved. "Argh!"

Mitch fell inside the barrel, sending it wobbling back and forth.

"Arrrrrrgh!" The boat thrashed in the water as Big Mo charged Patty Cannon's men.

He's going after them!

"Ya have him, Moses. Damn, I know ya have him!" The voice spiked from the shore.

"I don't got no poor nigger and I'm not lettin' you thieves on my boat. Argh!"

Mitch struggled to hold the barrel in place as the boat lobbed toward the voices on the shore.

BOOM!

"You crazy, Moses!?" Joe Johnson screamed. "No nigger, no matter how big, kin shoot at a white man an' live to talk 'bout it."

BOOM!

Mitch heard the men scatter up the bank.

"Come an' git me and I'll be feedin' ya to LizzieBeth!" Big Mo's words shot over the river as he walked across the deck. His footsteps stopped above Mitch's hiding place. "Stay put 'till I tell ya to move," he whispered through the hatch.

BOOM!

Mitch's sweat pooled on the floor under the stuffy barrel. He knew not to speak and closed his eyes to avoid the beads trickling over his lids. It seemed like hours passed before Big Mo opened the hatch and stooped into the small compartment to pull the barrel up and over Mitch.

"Ya done good. Ya knelt like I said." Big Mo led Mitch out of the compartment and to the deck of the boat. "Stretch yer legs an sit there by the wall, where no one kin see ya."

Mitch did as he was told and sat on the deck of the boat with his back to the wall of the ship. Big Mo rolled lengths of weighty hemp rope into a pile on the deck.

His biceps are bigger than my thighs.

The huge man wiped his hands on his bare chest, pulled dried jerky from a sack tied to his waist, and handed Mitch a chunk. "Boy, ya'll be leavin' here for the north."

"Who will take me from here?" Mitch had already bitten into the jerky, so talked with his mouth full.

"No one here to take ya. Ya'll need to go aways on yer own."

"But, I don't know where to go. I don't even know where I am. Can't I go with you?"

"Ha! Only if ya wants to go back south, stead of the north." He chewed his jerky. "I'll be crossin' the river to pick up some timber to haul back to Best Pitch. Got to make a livin' ya know."

Mitch wiped more sweat from his face and swatted a nagging mosquito. Neither Big Mo nor Mitch spoke until a great blue heron flew out of the water reeds and squawked, breaking the uncomfortable silence. "Where do I go?"

Big Mo finished his jerky and slid down the wall to sit alongside Mitch. His index finger drew an imaginary line on the deck. "Ya's here, at the northern end of the Transquakin'. Ya needs to git to here, to a little white chapel church near East New Market."

Mitch studied the imaginary line. "But, that's not a very long line." He traced the line with his own finger.

"Well, that would be 'causin ya don't have far to go right away. On a count of it's daytime. Ya needs to get yerself to a safe spot where ya kin hide until the moon is high in the sky. Right now, ya need to git yerself to this here church, where I knows it's safe to hide in the daytime."

Mitch rubbed his throbbing temples. "Mr. Ross told me I could find help in Cambridge. Can't I go there instead?"

Big Mo shook his head. "Ya caint go near Cambridge now. The Cannon woman will have her do-nothins crawlin' all over that city lookin' fer ya. I say ya go east, far from Cambridge."

Mitch cringed. "How do I get to the church by myself?"

Big Mo put his finger back on the deck. "Ya starts here. By getting off'n this boat. Then, ya travel up the Transquakin.'" He described the route, which would carry Mitch past a pond and to a small summer stream.

"Ya follow this here stream to a lumber yard. Stay in the reeds and watch our fer them beaver traps. They set them at low tide."

"Beaver traps?"

Big Mo spoke through his chewed jerky. "Beaver's the best eatin' meat there is. It don't eat critters itself, so its flesh is sweet as honey."

Mitch wrinkled his nose and Big Mo continued. "At that lumber yard, where the big logs are kept, ya needs to keep low and head toward the woods that hem the side of the yard. Run fer them woods and stay walkin' in 'em straight and north until they end at a cemetery. That there is the cemetery for the chapel." He thumped the deck with his finger.

"What if someone sees me at the lumber yard?"

"They cain't, else yer dead." Big Mo moved his finger from the cemetery as if it were making the trip itself. "Now, ya can rest a bit in the cemetery if ya like, but if'n it was me runnin', I'd head for the chapel and stay there. Being it's not a day of worship, ya shouldn't be havin any church folk disturbin ya."

Mitch focused on the imaginary line, trying to absorb the plan. He thought of his coach's words.

Dream, Plan, Work. This is a plan.

"By the time the night comes, ya'll be itchin' to run. I'm tellin' ya now. Stay put and don't be runnin' until after that first owl screeches. Make sure the sky is good 'n dark, then be on yer way."

"But, I don't know where to go from there."

"I thought ya told me ya was goin' north. Be on yer way north then!" Big Mo's finger thumped the deck.

Mitch drew his legs in close to his chest. "But, sir, how do I get there? North, I mean."

The last bite of jerky slid down Big Mo's throat. "Hold it now, boy. Ain't you never followed the stars?"

Mitch closed his eyes and rubbed the greasy hair on his scalp. The idea was familiar to him. A song he learned in fifth grade history fluttered in his head.

Left foot, peg foot, traveling on. Follow the Drinking Gourd.

"You mean, the constellations, the Big Dipper? The Drinking Gourd in the stars?"

Big Mo smiled. "Yessir. Them stars will never fail ya, as long as ya follow them properly. Clouds and storms and such might mess ya up a bit. But, the bright star won't fail ya none." His finger slid back to the deck and traced another line, this one curved like a fishing hook.

"Ya see here is the gourd neck and right off'n that neck is the brightest star in the sky." The finger thumped the deck again. "That's the star ya follow."

The two gazed at the imaginary star on the deck. Suddenly, Big Mo rumbled to his feet and yanked on the boat's sail ropes. "Ya got to go while nobody's on the river." He pulled a fat chunk of jerky from the bag at his waist and tossed it to Mitch.

"Now?" Mitch caught the jerky and hurriedly stood up himself, wiping the dust from his rough trousers. He tripped over a rope on the deck and clumsily dropped the jerky into his sack with the remaining biscuits. "Do I have to go right *now*?"

Big Mo faced Mitch. "When ya run, ya run fast as soon as the way clears before ya. Ya don't be waitin' to eat, or to rest or to even be doing yer business in the woods. Ya just run becuzzin ya can." He raised his muscular arm over his head and brought it down like a horse whip to his side. "Git!"

Mitch dashed to the side of the boat and tossed one leg over. "Yes. Yes, sir!" He tossed the other leg over and heaved his body into the marshes along the shore. He splashed into murky water to his knees and called back to Big Mo. "Sir? I need to know one thing. Just one more thing."

Big Mo stood on the deck with his blistered and calloused hands on his hips.

Mitch stuttered. "What about LizzieBeth? How do I keep her away from me?"

"Ha!" Big Mo's guffaw shook the boat. "Ya worry about that Patty Cannon witch and I'll take care of LizzieBeth. Now git!"

Mitch rushed ahead and stumbled through the reeds and up the bank. As he made his way from Big Mo's boat, a lone piece of fresh parchment paper blew over the ground before him. Mitch reached for the paper as it fluttered up the hill. He grabbed it, landed on his belly, and gasped as he read the large print scrawled across the single sheet:

One Hundred Dollars Reward

Runaway from the Subscriber one boy named Mitchey, Age about 13 years. He is very fair of color, almost passing for white, about 5 feet eight inches height.

One hundred dollars reward will be given for the above negroe, if taken out of state, and $50 if taken in the state.

Patty Cannon
Near Johnsons Crossroads, Delaware
August 1823

Chapter 22
Friday Afternoon.

"Dodo Mitch. Mitchell, wake up." Annie shook his shoulder. "It looks like you're going to kill yourself on this chair."

Mitch opened his eyes and jerked his head forward, his reflexes slapping his arms to his side. "What? What do you want?"

"Hey, I'm going to Meghan's house so you get to go to the library by yourself. Lucky boy."

"What? What time is it?" Mitch swung his legs off the lounge.

"Lunchtime!" She shoved an ice cream bar in his face. "Come on. Mrs. Mulbry said she'll drop you on the way."

"At the library?"

"Duh. And guess what? You get to swim in the A meet on Saturday!"

"What?" The fog lifted and Mitch sprang to his feet. "I've never swam in an A meet before. I'm a B meet swimmer! How do you know I'm swimming in the A meet?"

"Whoa. Daryl told me, and you'll do great. You rocked in freestyle the other night. You can do it!"

Mitch groaned and followed Annie out of the pool area. As they passed the guardhouse she waved goodbye to Daryl. He, in turn, shot both Mitch and Annie a thumbs-up.

DEAD: Daryl, Stupid Swim Coach, Age 19

Mitch rode in silence with the Mulbrys to the library, entered the stubborn automatic door and, once inside, turned left to sign in for the computers, trying to avoid Mrs. Docent's glare.

At the desk, he fumbled for a pen, giving the volunteer ample opportunity to draw her glasses to her nose to get a good look at his signature, and at him.

"Mitchell Burke, is it?" Her lips curled. "I believe I have worked with you, but I have never had the pleasure of officially meeting you." She leaned forward on the desk, one arm supporting her substantial weight as she extended her other towards Mitch. "You are the Internet boy, are you not? How do you do, Mr. Burke? I am Mrs. Sharpe."

Oh, God. How does she know my name?

He slowly extended his hand. "Uh, nice to meet you, Mrs. um, Sharpe." Mrs. Docent pumped Mitch's hand once, then twice, and then turned her attention back to the sign-in sheet.

"Are you here to conduct research, Mr. Burke?"

"Yes, ma'am. I am."

"Really?" drawled Mrs. Docent. "How very interesting." She peered at Mitch. "Just what are you researching, young man?"

Mitch stood, fully exposed to Mrs. Docent's glare. "I'm studying, um..." He paused and drew his hands out of his pockets, leaving them dangling like puppet arms.

"The Underground Railroad. In, um, Maryland."

Mrs. Docent raised her pencil-thin eyebrows. "The Underground Railroad?"

"Yes, ma'am. I'm…interviewing descendants of slaves from Maryland."

Slave descendants? Where am I going to find one of those?

"Brilliant!" Mrs. Docent exclaimed. "Primary source research. You're going right to the source."

Mitch coughed into his hand.

"I'll tell you what, dear. Why don't you take an extra twenty minutes at the terminal today?"

"Uh, thank you Mrs. Do-, Mrs. Sharpe, ma'am."

Mrs. Docent smiled like a lizard on a warm patio as Mitch slithered to the computer room. At the terminal, he concentrated on his screen. He opened his email and checked his inbox. It was empty.

Nothing from Dad.

He plunked at the keys and created a short message.

Hi Dad. I know you're not going to get this for a while, but I thought I'd send anyway. You were right about Harriet Tubman. I'm on my own.

Mitch sat back from the screen.

Bad news can distract soldiers in combat.

He leaned forward.

But I'm ok. I hope you're safe. Love, Mitch

Click.

Mitch rested his head in his hands.

What do I do now?

He sat on his hands and took a minute to think.

Global Search. Underground Railroad.

He opened a search engine and typed "Underground Railroad." The screen scrolled with options before him:

Results 1-10 of about 32,000 for Underground Railroad.

Underground Railroad: History of Slavery, Pictures, Information

Underground Railroad: Special Resource Study

Aboard the Underground Railroad

Where do I start?

With a quick click, Mitch opened "Aboard the Underground Railroad." The first page of text opened and he eagerly read, looking for escape routes to Canada.

What route did they follow?

He jumped from the first site to the next.

"Underground Railroad History"

And then to the next.

"Underground Railroad—An American History Movement"

None of the sites gave him a specific route from Maryland's Eastern Shore to Canada. He scrolled through pages of Underground Railroad information until, at last, he came to a site called, "The Routes of the Underground Railroad."

"Alright!" he blurted.

He opened the site and was immediately disappointed. The map that lay before him was the same one in his July 1984 *National Geographic* article. Thick orange lines curved and sprawled over an 1860 map of the United States. Arrows showed major, but not detailed, avenues of escape.

God, they ran from everywhere.

Slaves escaped from as far south as Georgia, Alabama, Mississippi, and Louisiana, making their way to free Canada between the east coast and the northern Great Lakes states. Some slaves from Texas and northern Florida ran to freedom in Mexico and the Caribbean. The lands west of Minnesota, Missouri, and Arkansas were still territories, some unorganized. Mitch read the sidebar information, written in very small print around the edges of the map.

"None of this matters!" He zeroed in on the map of Maryland, but couldn't find any detail. "How do I get to Canada? Ugh!" He exhaled his irritation.

"May I help you?" Mrs. Sharpe appeared out of nowhere and moved her red glasses up her nose as she spoke.

"I can't find a route from Maryland to Canada." Mitch said. "I need one for my report."

Mrs. Sharpe smiled. "That's why I'm here."

"Oh." He squirmed.

"Actually, I don't think there is such a thing as a detailed map for the Underground Railroad." She chuckled. "It's not likely Triple A routed slaves."

This time, Mitch smiled.

Mrs. Sharpe turned and cleared *Underground Railroad* from Mitch's search screen. "Do an advanced search. Type 'Quakers and the Underground Railroad.'"

Mitch did as he was told and within seconds a dozen sites sprang up in front of him.

"See?" She pointed to his screen. "One of these sites will tell you where the big Quaker colonies were. Where there were Quakers, there were runaway slaves. Mrs. Sharpe walked back and sat down at her desk. He lifted his hand in a weak wave and then settled back to his screen.

DEAD: Mitchell Thomas Burke: Stupid, Stupid, Age 13

Chapter 23

Friday Night at Home. Secrets Divulged.

Mitch walked the two miles from the library and arrived home to see his mom's van in the driveway. Fritzi barked from the porch next door as he entered the house.

"Mitchell? Mitchell, is that you?" Mrs. Burke asked from the den.

Mitch sighed. "Yeah mom, it's me."

"Is Annie with you, my 'A meet' swimmer boy?" She walked from the den towards the kitchen, tapping Mitch on the shoulder as she passed.

"Who told you?" Mitch dropped his swim bag and followed her into the kitchen. "I am not swimming the A meet!"

His mom lifted the lid on the slow cooker and stirred the steamy chicken-tomato concoction. "Can I take that as a 'No, Annie is not with me, Mom'?"

He slouched against the wall. "Come on, Mom."

"What's wrong with swimming in the A meet?" She took plates out of the cupboard and glanced at the flicking ceramic tail of the clock. "Where do you think your sister is? She was supposed to be home from Meghan's by now." She stacked the plates on the counter.

"Mom...Will you listen to me? I don't want to swim in the A meet. I don't even want to stay on swim team."

"Mitchell, that's silly. You're turning into a great swimmer and you deserve to swim in the A meets." She tossed lettuce into the sink and turned on the water.

"I hate it."

"Since when have you hated it? You've loved to swim since you were a baby."

"I'm not a baby anymore. And, I don't want to swim on a team named the Ladybugs. It's embarrassing." Mitch sat on the counter stool. "And, it's stupid."

"Is that what this is all about? You're embarrassed of the team name?" She stopped washing lettuce and dried her hands. "Or, is there something else?"

"Nothing else." He squirmed in his seat.

His mom rested her elbows on the counter top. "Let me tell you the story of the ladybug. It's quite a nifty little creature."

"Ah, come on Mom…" Mitch rolled his eyes to the ceiling.

"As the story goes, years ago in medieval Europe aphids were totally destroying the crops. These teeny, tiny bugs were decimating the food supply for the entire continent. Without food, people would die by the thousands. Probably tens of thousands. Maybe even more. Can you imagine all of those people dying at the same time?"

"Mom, the story."

"Okay. So anyway, townspeople everywhere decided they needed to pray to Our Lady, the Virgin Mary, as a last ditch effort. Nothing else had worked."

"This is not going to be a religion lesson, is it?"

"A little religion could do you some good, young man."

"Okay, okay. I'm sorry. What about the story?"

"So all of these poor, starving people prayed to Our Lady day and night for a long time. In response to their prayers, she sent millions of bugs to eat the aphids. They came in swarms and saved the crops. The farmers called them 'the beetles of Our Lady.' Hence, 'ladybug!'"

Mitch looked at his mother's face. "Mom, you're beaming."

"Don't you see how special these creatures are? You should be proud to swim on behalf of such a strong bug!"

"You're kidding."

"So, Mitchell. Ladybugs are a sign of good luck. And, never, ever kill one." She patted the lettuce dry and began to rip it into the salad bowl.

"Got it." He was eager to change the subject. "Mom, can I ask a kind of personal question?"

"As long as it has nothing to do with the men I dated before I met your father. I hate it when you and your sister ask me those questions." She glanced at the clock. "Where is she? She was supposed to be home 30 minutes ago."

"Mom…"

"Okay. What's the question?"

Mitch scratched his head and shifted in his seat. "Did Dad, ever go through a, um, vulnerable time in his life? You know, where he was real worried, or scared, or something like that?"

Mrs. Burke looked directly at Mitch. "What are you asking?"

Mitch hesitated, then rambled. "Well, I always thought Dad was super strong…and was never scared. But, he told me he went through a really awful time 13 years ago. Then we got cut off on the phone. He couldn't explain what he started to tell me."

Mitch's mom twisted the towel in her hands and didn't speak.

"Mom?" Mitch leaned on the counter.

She sighed and placed the rolled up towel in front of him. "I wasn't planning on telling you for a little more time. But, I suppose if your father brought it up, I'll tell you."

"What?"

"When you were born, we had some difficulties. It was a very tough time for your father." She opened the slow cooker lid and stirred the partially cooked chicken. Mitch waited for her to continue her story.

"I'm still not sure if now is the time to talk about this. I would prefer to explain this with your father at my side." Her voice cracked and she kept her eyes on the steaming dinner.

"That's not fair. Dad might not be back for awhile."

Click, Clock, Click, Clock.

He listened to the rooster clock count down his mom's thoughts. Finally, she spoke. "Mitchell, when you were born the birth did not go well."

"You mean, I got hurt?"

"Actually, *I* did."

Mitch pulled his elbows off the counter. "What do you mean you got hurt?"

"Just that. I delivered you, a healthy baby, and then suffered a stroke post delivery. I spent the next three weeks in the hospital. After that, I was in physical and occupational therapy for many months."

"You mean you almost died and I was fine? Why didn't you ever tell me that?"

"Calm down, honey." She reached across the counter and touched Mitch's arm. "We weren't hiding anything from you. We just wanted to tell you when we knew you could handle the information."

"What's there to handle? I was born healthy and you almost died. Simple. I almost killed you."

"Now there you go with the theatrics. The stroke could've happened to anyone and frankly, I was darned lucky."

Mitch frowned.

Mom almost died.

"Look, I don't want to argue with you about this. It was a rotten time for us—especially for your father. But, we got through it and are now very fortunate to have such a healthy family."

Dad almost lost Mom. Patty Cannon stalked him when he was afraid that Mom was going to die.

"What did Dad do?"

"Your father took leave from the military and took care of both of us."

"Wow, that must have been hard."

"It was. He didn't sleep for months." She eased back into preparing the salad.

For months? Did Patty chase him for months?

"For months?"

"Yup. For months."

"Did he ever...get over it?" Mitch tossed a wayward piece of lettuce into the bowl.

"Get over it? Jeez, I never thought of your dad 'getting over it.' It certainly changed him. Made him more cautious...and definitely more protective! He used to sit up at night by your crib when he couldn't sleep."

Dad was making sure she wasn't coming after me.

"So, anyway, I'm fine. Dad's fine, and we're all fine. Right?" She plunked the bowl of salad in front of Mitch and said, "Taste this."

Mitch slowly reached for the salad bowl. "Mom, that's why you adopted Annie, isn't it? You couldn't have any more kids."

"That's right. Now taste."

The conversation was over.

BANG!

The mudroom door flew open with hurricane force and Annie blew in. "I'm home!"

Mitch retracted his hand without tasting the salad and said, "It's fine."

Mrs. Burke whizzed past Mitch and headed Annie off at the stairs. "Anna Maria! Why are you so late? I asked you to be home almost an hour ago. And, it's six thirty right now, young lady."

"It's *six thirty*? My watch says five thirty! Look." She thrust her wrist in her mom's direction as she put her pool bag on the stairs.

Mrs. Burke's admonition was short-lived and the three went on to eat a pleasant meal together. Afterwards, Annie convinced her mother to leave the clean up to her and Mitch and take a walk in the neighborhood. A happy Mrs. Burke exited the house and gently shut the door behind her.

Immediately, Annie zoomed by her brother on the way to the stairs. "Stay here. I have something to show you!" She returned in a few minutes carrying her empty pool bag, a massive pile of CDs, and a portable CD player.

"Look!" She rolled them out of her arms onto the tabletop.

Mitch eyed the messy pile and read: *Relaxation for Swimmers, Deep Breathing for a Healthier Life,* and *Think Positive Thoughts*

"Annie, what is this?"

She shook out her excitement by twisting and dancing alongside the table.

"I got Meghan's sister to take us back to the pool on the way home. That's why I was so late. I asked Daryl if I could borrow these cool relaxation CDs." She reached across the table and grabbed the CD player. "And look! He lent me his brand-new, water resistant, CD player. Cool, huh?"

Mitch flipped through the CDs. "What makes you think I need, or even *want*, for that matter, to listen to these? I don't think it's relaxation I need."

"Sure it is, Mitch. She told me you just needed to relax. Unwind a bit." Annie pushed *Relaxation For Swimmers* towards Mitch. "See? Isn't this cool?"

"What are you talking about? Who told you I needed to relax?" He thought a minute. "You didn't tell Meghan or her sister about this, did you? I'll kill you if you did!"

Annie dashed to the opposite side of the table. "I'm not that stupid!"

"Then, who told you?"

"She did. When I took a nap at Meghan's. Patty did."

The rooster tail clicked once, then twice.

Mitch screamed, "Patty Cannon came to you in your dream!?"

Stunned, Annie nodded at her brother. "Mitch, she was nice."

Chapter 24

Later Friday Night. Looking for Fritzi.

"What do you mean she was nice? Are you crazy? She was a murderer!"

"She was nice, Mitch. She just talked to me, *nicely*." Annie looked down at her feet. "And she's worried about you."

"Worried about me?" Mitch roared. "She wants to kill me!"

"Stop it, you're scaring me." Annie backed away from the table.

"Since when have I ever scared you?"

"With this stuff. With all this Patty Cannon stuff. It scares me!" Tears welled up in Annie's round eyes.

Mitch lowered his voice. "Okay, look. You didn't believe her, did you? I mean, you never told her she was right or anything, did you?"

"No. I never talked to her. Meghan woke me up before I could ever speak."

"Good. That's good, I think." He walked to the sink and poured himself a glass of water, which he stared into as he drank slowly. "Annie," he turned to face her, "you can't let her get you. Don't believe a word she says."

Annie held her tears back. "I'm scared. Can't we tell Mom?"

"You can't be scared." Mitch stood by his sister and put a hand on her shoulder. "And no, you can't tell Mom. Just don't let Patty Cannon get you. Be strong."

"You're the strong one, not me."

Knock.

Knock. Knock.

"What's that?" Mitch put his finger to his lips.

"I didn't hear anything."

Knock.

Knock. Knock.

"Someone's at the door," Mitch whispered.

"Are you sure? That's the littlest knock I've ever heard."

Mitch left the kitchen and followed the sound to the mudroom. He opened the door to find Pete Kimmel, the seven year-old boy from next door, standing on the stairs. His skinny legs protruded out from under a long pair of plaid shorts and his auburn hair was perfectly slicked and combed to the left.

"Hey, Petey. What's up?"

"Hello." Pete looked up at his neighbors with a face as blank as a white sheet of copy paper.

"Do you need something, Petey?"

Pete squashed a bug with his foot, keeping his eyes on the gooey orange spot. Mitch watched the spot, too, and shuddered.

"Yo, Pete!" Annie grew impatient. "Do you want to come in or something?"

"No."

"Did your mom send you here for something?"

Pete looked up at Mitch. "Could you please come with me to the creek in the woods? Fritzi is missing and we think he might be there. My mom said I couldn't go without a *responsible* party."

He must've practiced saying that word.

Mitch smiled at Annie. "I guess that would be us. Sure we'll go, Petey."

"Wait a second," Annie pointed her finger at Pete. "Did you guys pray to Saint Anthony first?"

"Saint Anthony?" Pete asked.

"Leave him alone. I don't think the Kimmels pray to saints."

"Why not?"

"They're not Catholic."

"Well, it's not like we have a lock on praying to saints."

"Annie, lay off."

"Okay then, I'll go write mom a note telling her where we are."

While Annie wrote Mrs. Burke a note in the house, Mitch spoke to Pete, who was tracking bugs crawling on the asphalt driveway. "How long has Fritzi been gone?"

"I think all day. He wasn't there when I got home from camp."

"But, I heard him barking when I came home."

"Really?" Pete said. "Nobody else has seen him." He narrowed his hunt to one panicked ladybug that rested on the bottom stone step to the house. He lifted his shoe up high, aiming to annihilate the bug.

Mitch swirled on the steps and grabbed Pete's foot. "Don't step on that!"

"Why not?"

"Because they're good luck. Never squash good luck." Mitch placed Pete's foot down next to the bug.

"Okay, Mitch," Pete whispered.

"Let's go." Annie bound out of the house. "I'll lead the way."

Mitch stood up from the steps. "No, I will. Come on Pete."

"Whatever." She followed Mitch and Pete across the backyard to the woods.

The summer night sky screamed heat, haze, and brilliant colors. Sparrows swooped through wisps of lavender and orange as Mitch, Annie, and Pete looked for Fritzi. After an hour of whistling and calling for the dog, Mitch decided it was time to get Pete home. Afterwards, they entered their own house and found Mrs. Burke in the den, engrossed in the evening news. She clicked off the war coverage when the two walked in the room.

"Any luck finding Fritzi?"

"None." Annie flopped on the leather sofa next to her mother and Mitch stood to search the shelves for the *National Geographic* Magazine he had tucked away. Finding it, he pulled it down from between his dad's books.

"Too bad." His mom said. "That hot-dog drives me nuts, but I know it's little Pete's best friend. Let's hope he turns up."

"Yeah, lets hope the mailman didn't stuff him into a delivery box. He hates that dog!"

"Annie! Have some mercy." Mrs. Burke stood and stretched. "At least a little." She closed her eyes, sighed, and then reopened them. "Guys, your exciting mom is going to take a bath and read a book."

"Okay." Mitch spoke with his back to his mother and his eyes locked on the open magazine.

"What are you looking for, Mitchell? She approached him and peeked over his shoulder. "Are you still doing research for your report?"

"Um, yeah. I'm looking up Quakers."

"Of course. How's the written work going?"

Mitch changed the subject. "You look tired tonight, Mom."

Annie nodded her agreement.

Mrs. Burke yawned and said, "Good night, then." She blew her children kisses and climbed the stairs to her bedroom. Minutes later, bathtub water ran through the pipes in the walls.

Annie stretched out on the couch. "Actually, a hot bath sounds good. Maybe I'll take one too."

"Nothing doing." Mitch pulled her up from her resting space. "Come on. We need to prepare you for tonight."

"What do you mean, 'for tonight?'" Annie followed her brother up the stairs. They tiptoed by their mother's closed door and ended in Mitch's room.

He shut the door behind them and motioned for Annie to sit on his rumpled bed.

"I've been thinking. We have to make sure that you don't dream about Patty Cannon again." He pulled a pile of *Cosmic Comics* off his bookshelves. "Here, start with these," he said, plopping 107 through 114 in her lap.

"What are you talking about? What am I supposed to do with these, swat at her?"

Mitch sat beside Annie. "Look, I think you can avoid her if you fill your head with 'light' stuff before you go to sleep. Happy stuff."

"Why don't you do that?" She thumbed through the comic books.

"I have a plan, and I'm going to work it. Just do what I say."

"Okay, okay. But here…" Annie pulled the small plastic bag of roasted and salted peanuts from her pocket and handed it to Mitch. "If I can focus on comics, you can will these into your dream, at least. You need to keep up your energy." The dancing Peanut Man smiled up at Mitch.

"Okay. I'll do it this time."

Annie slipped off the bed and tiptoed to the door, turning before she opened it. "Mitch? I didn't tell you something. Josiah was there. He was with her."

"What? Why didn't you tell me that?"

She clenched her fists. "There you go! You're screaming at me again. You're scaring me!"

"Shh!" He inhaled deeply. "Sorry." And exhaled. "Did he say anything?"

Annie shook her head. "No." She paused. "And Mitch, you never told me he was crippled."

"Crippled?"

Stay calm. Don't scare her.

"What do you mean?"

"His legs. They're wrapped in bandages."

Mitch's heart pounded.

What did she do to him?

He stared at his sister.

She has to go to bed happy.

"Oh that…that's probably just to…keep his legs warm." He put the peanuts on his bed and fumbled through his stack of comic books. "Now, go read what you have and let me know what you think of number 114."

Mitch escorted Annie to her own room.

"Good night."

Normally she liked her door shut.

"Goodnight, bro."

But this time, he left it open a crack…just in case she screamed in the middle of the night.

Chapter 25
Finding the Chapel.

Long after Annie and his mom fell asleep, Mitch sat on the edge of his bed holding the bag of peanuts and reading his scribbled notes on the *National Geographic* article. He searched for hidden clues he might have missed before. His eyes concentrated on the college-ruled page while his ears concentrated on Annie's room.

Not a sound. If she makes a sound, I'm going to wake her up.

He read the notes over in order to imprint them on his brain:

Slavery, "The Peculiar Institution."
Slaves escaped years before it was called The
Underground Railroad.

Before he reached the bottom of the page, Mitch fell asleep on top of his covers.

The sun bore down on his face and he woke, clutching the piece of parchment paper that, in five lines, defined him as a runaway:

One Hundred Dollars Reward

Still lying on his belly, Mitch looked down the muddy bank.

Stay in the reeds. Work the plan. Big Mo said to stay in the reeds.

He crammed the runaway notice into the biscuit sack inside his shirt and slid down to safety. Once sheltered by the tall and sticky grasses, Mitch ran in the direction Big Mo drew on the deck.

Take the stream to the lumberyard, to the woods, to the cemetery, to the chapel.

The reeds whipped Mitch's body and he forged ahead, working into a steady gait and rhythmically swatting reeds and pussy willows from his path.

Watch for beaver traps. Watch your feet.

Mitch flew, but every so often, stumbled. Swallows swooped above him, nipping at the marsh. Above the swallows, he could make out a pair of buzzards, lazily circling in the blue sky. He slowed down.

I have such a headache.

Heat seared Mitch's shoulders as the dense marsh thinned out. He crouched between the reeds, swallowed what little spit was left in his mouth, and saw the river end in a murky pond before him. A lumberyard sat on the eastern edge of the pond.

"Thank you, God."

Huge logs, some fifty feet long, straddled each other in pile upon pile. Some were stripped bare, while others supported limb remnants hanging from them, like broken arms. Chains wrapped the more unwieldy trunks, as if restraining them so they wouldn't escape. They looked like shackles on slaves.

Mitch followed the pond bank closer to the yard. He was dizzy and his headache throbbed.

"Get to the woods. I'll be okay in the woods."

Vibrant green trees swayed in the distance. Mitch stayed undercover and scrambled between reeds until he reached the woods. His muscles ached and sweat ran off his forehead to his lips. The salt hit his tongue and reminded him that his troubles were very, very real. He crawled into the woods and, once inside the shadows of the trees, felt inside his shirt for his sack of biscuits, jerky, and his runaway notice.

Crinkle. Crinkle.

Somehow, the crinkle of the notice soothed his frayed nerves. Mitch felt for the notice again.

Crinkle.

Inside the sack, his hand wrapped around plastic, not paper.

The peanuts. I've got Annie's peanuts!

He tucked in his shirt and staggered forward. Mitch stayed "north and straight" like Big Mo had ordered, stopping to rub the huge trunks as he passed them.

North. Moss grows on the north side of a tree.

The feel of the plush moss comforted Mitch, as did the damp underbrush. His wild heart rate slowed, beat-by-beat, to almost, but not quite, normal. He breathed in the cool air and the chirps of the flitting red cardinals swirled in his head, dancing in and out of his headache.

Mitch stopped to get his bearings and rest against a pine tree. The sunlight streaked through the trees, illuminating a huge white sycamore glowing under a clear blue sky in the distance. He had reached the end of the forest. Mitch pushed himself off of the tree and out into a meadow. The massive sycamore, its bark peeling in sheets, glimmered and towered over the grounds of a small white chapel and its cemetery.

Mitch's head pounded. He fixed his burning eyes to the ground and swayed toward the cemetery. The white chapel sat just across the field of graves, but appeared an eternity away to Mitch. His world was starting to spin and he was losing focus on the pristine building. Soon, the cemetery engulfed him, stone after stone screaming names of the deceased.

Dead: John Anthony Blake
Dead: Margaret Elizabeth Ball
Dead: Zachariah Doon

Mitch's clothes stuck to his body with sweat. He faced the chapel and placed his right foot in front of his left.

Dead: Emma Louise Halloway
Dead: Burke Sharpe

Drops of sweat landed on a polished headstone. Mitch's heart drummed in his ears and he rushed away from the graves. His arms hung heavy as he weaved and stumbled through the grass, the straight lines of the chapel blurring in the distance. Uneven rows of deep depressions sank in the ground before Mitch. He wobbled around them, avoiding them, desperately trying to see the chapel, his head pounding, and his fever overtaking his vision.

The pits in the earth pursued him as the cloud wisps and buzzards swirled above him. He fell to his knees, then forward on his belly, landing in a depression about two feet deep into the earth.

"St. Anthony," he gasped. "Please. Help me. Find. The chapel."

The length of his body fit perfectly into the cool hole and he fell unconscious, only after realizing that he had fallen into a sunken, unmarked grave.

Chapter 26
Finding the Quakers.

"Now that the boy is settled, Samuel, tell me his story. He appears to be a boy of some means. And, dare I say, of little color. Much lighter in complexion than even the boys of the Willis family, who are of mixed blood and take respite here as well."

A firm, but soft, voice floated over Mitch. His heart thumped at the back of his throat, but he kept his eyes shut.

"I do not know much of his story, sir. As I soon discovered him face down in a wretched Negro grave in a Caroline County churchyard."

A piece of paper crinkled.

"On his body lay this fugitive notice, as it were. Along with a curious item or two. He goes by the name, 'Mitchey.' Seemingly, the Johnson gang is in pursuit of this child."

"My good Lord. The man-hunters feed the hell of American slavery."

"He has been quite ill the days since, and I have transported him from that site to the Jenkins estate in Camden, to here."

A coarse hand brushed Mitch's hair from his forehead.

"It were Mrs. Jenkins who tended to the boy's fever and better suited him in attire fitting of a white lad."

Mitch stirred in a bed of straw.

"Ah, so it was that my cousin, Mr. Jenkins, has sent along a note explaining the arrival of his *nephew*, in thy due care."

Mitch rolled to his back.

They're helping me.

Samuel chuckled. "Yes, sir. A white lad traveling with a colored man-servant to his Uncle Charles' residence. So it were that we passed the constables en route."

"Samuel, thee is sly, and a trophy to thy community." Charles Law responded.

Mitchell opened his eyes to see two distinguished men, one white and one black, looking over his bed of straw. The white gentleman had a smooth, kind face and wore black trousers and suspenders. His white shirtsleeves were rolled to his elbows and his dark brown hair curled about his ears.

The black gentleman was taller, and much better dressed. He wore a dark green waistcoat that matched well with his soft grey trousers, and held a green felt cap in his hands. He smiled, yet had a serious tone about him. He spoke to Mitch first. "Good day, lad. Are you well?"

Mitch slowly sat up and took in his surroundings. He was in a simple but spacious barn, devoid of animals. Across the barn sat an entire family, in the straw where the cows would have laid, near a large back door. A mother, father, and four children. They huddled together and listened intently to the conversation.

They must be the Willis family.

The boys had the complexion of their mother—light brown and even. The father's skin was darker and worn, evidence of his time spent in the harsh outdoors. Mitch looked down at himself and felt the fine linen shirt, which he now wore. Dyed brown cotton slacks had replaced his burlap trousers, and he wore leather shoes on his feet.

He sat, with his hands in the straw, and felt for the sack that Mary had given him. It now hung by a fresh leather strap from a loop on his trousers. He squeezed the sack until he felt Annie's peanuts, careful not to let the bag crinkle this time. Satisfied, he brought his attention back to the two men, who were waiting patiently for a reply.

"I, I am well, thank you." He felt his bony wrists and realized he hadn't been well at all. "I mean, I feel okay. I think I'm well."

Charles Law spoke. "Son, it appears thee is a fugitive, yet are in fine company." He patted Samuel on the back. "Thee has received the benefit and assistance of the most brave colored man in the state of Delaware. Friend Burns here risks his freedom in the spirit of righteousness."

Samuel Burns said nothing, and neither did Mitch, so Charles continued.

"It appears to me thee is of better health and able to continue a journey north, afar from the slave-hunters."

"Are you a Quaker?" Mitch blurted.

The two men glanced at each other and smiled. Charles said, "Aye, I am a Friend, son. And Friend Burns is a friend of a Friend." He chuckled at his own joke.

Mitch flushed with embarrassment. "I'm sorry. I just have never met a Quaker before."

"There and then, thee must have traveled from the far south. Ha!" Charles laughed out loud.

Samuel took the opportunity to interject. "Lad, over due time, the Johnson gang will be following. Are you able to continue a journey north? If so, Mr. Law will write you a letter of introduction as his relation that should enable you to travel unencumbered."

Mitch was taken by Samuel Burn's perfect diction and speech. "Sir, are you a slave?"

Samuel, holding his cap at his waist, responded, "No, child. I was born into freedom, but have yet to see the day when my liberties are not challenged." He paused. "You question my speech. I was educated by a minister's wife who took it upon herself to change the world, God rest her soul."

"And to this day," Charles said, "Friend Burns is a better read man than I." He turned to Samuel. "The Johnson gang makes regular pursuit in these environs. I suggest the child go forth at present, and the Willis family will follow."

"I do indeed sense the trouble myself." Samuel looked down at Mitch. "I suggest we depart via carriage this evening, after we have the opportunity to allay our weariness."

"Enough be said. Son, we will bring satisfying food shortly. Thee will remain in the barn, out of sight of the Johnson gang." Mitch nodded his approval and Charles escorted Samuel to the door. "Samuel, as my cousin's good friend, thee might take supper in the kitchen and rest by the fire."

The two men exited the barn, leaving Mitch and the Willis family behind shut doors.

The boy is staring at me.

"Hello," he muttered, half-hoping that was all the communication he needed to deliver.

"Hallo!" The older boy, about ten years old, jumped up from his sleeping family and rushed across the barn to Mitch's side. "Ya a house boy? Ya sho don't look like a field boy."

Mitch stayed in his straw pile. "I'm not a slave," he murmured.

"Ya ain't no slave, ya look like a white boy, and ya runnin'? What about a servant? Ya a paid servant?"

"I'm neither. I'm, I'm free. Patty Cannon wants me to be her slave."

"Patty Cannon!? How'd ya go 'bout gettin' in her way?" The boy sat on the dirt floor next to Mitch, and crossed his arms, exposing the letter "S" burned into his bicep.

"What's that?" Mitch reached out to the scar.

"Ya never seen brandin' before?" The boy turned his arm in Mitch's direction.

"You were branded, like a cow?"

"An' it hurt like the Lord Jesus done felt." He ran his right finger over his left bicep. "S" is for slave. An' I ain't no slave neither. My pappy has free papers on all o' us, signed by the old mistress. But, she died and no second mistress or no slave catcher cares what the paper say when the body say 'slave.'"

"Wow." Mitch couldn't take his eyes off the boy's arm.

"Ya should see my Pappy's back. He been whupped so many times his back don't look human. Looks like big fat snakes are restin' on his skin."

Mitch grimaced and glanced in the direction of the Willis family. The remaining children and the parents were curled in sleep. "Has your mother ever been hurt?"

The boy scrunched his dark pink lips before he spoke. "My momma's heart got torn and busted. My big sister Isabelle was done taken from Momma not too long ago an' sold to Georgia. That's why Pappy says it time to run. He don't want to lose the rest of us." The boy sat back.

Mitch fiddled with the straw, sitting in silence with the boy for some time. Finally, he spoke. "I'm sorry that your sister was sold. That must be pretty awful, having your sister sold away."

The boy sat, rubbing the "S" on his arm. "Yep. Sho is."

Just then, light poured in the barn as the door opened. The boy jumped up and ran like a rabbit back to his family. Mitch tried to burrow into his straw.

"Tis I," boomed Charles Law. He entered the barn, juggling three cloth-covered baskets in his arms. "Friend Law, my cherished wife, has put together a fine meal for our weary guests." He steadied the top basket with his chin and gingerly placed the three on a nearby barrel. He walked back to the barn door and shut it. "I fear the lack of a dining table in this barn, but I assume the good company and Lord's blessing will more than make up for poor atmosphere." He walked back to the food, and opened his arms to invite everyone to the bounty at the barrel.

Mitch smelled the bread and sausage and smiled across the room at the boy. The two simultaneously stood and approached the barrel. Mitch drew back the blue cloth, picked up the kitchen knife, and cut himself and the boy each a piece of hearty wheat bread. They stood at the barrel, eating chunks of bread and the juicy sausage.

As the Willis family woke—first the parents, then the other children—a voice from outside the barn pierced the calm.

"Mr. Law. Mr. Law! It's me, Constable Hardy. Are you in the barn, sir?"

The boys scattered back to their straw piles, the Willis boy whispering, "The Constable and the catchers done found us!"

Charles raised his finger to his lips and softly walked toward the Willis family, which was now quite awake. Mrs. Willis cupped her hands over the mouths of the youngest children and Mr. Willis pulled the boy and his brother close to his chest. Charles walked by the family and to the rear barn door. He quietly pushed it open as wide as his body and exited into the barnyard, closing the door behind him.

"Lord have mercy," breathed Mr. Willis. "Please don't split us up and have us be sold to every corner of the south." He rocked the two boys at his chest.

Charles called to the Constable from the back of the barn. "I am working in the barnyard, Friend Hardy. Can I be of service to thee?"

The Willis family and Mitch held their breath for what seemed like forever. The Constable spoke, this time from around back of the barn.

"Sir, we have come to inspect your home for fugitive activity on the premises."

"Friend, there are no fugitives in my house!" Charles spat back.

"The neighbors have reported activity, Mr. Law."

"Is thee in possession of a search warrant?"

A different, unrefined, and loud voice broke into the conversation. "Charles Law, we are here to claim our property!"

"It's Joe Johnson!" Mitch gasped. He jumped to his feet and moved, with the kitchen knife in hand, toward the front barn door.

Mr. Willis frantically motioned for him to stay quiet and sit down.

"They want me, not you!" In a single movement, Mitch opened the door, stepped outside, and shut the door behind him.

No more beatings. No more branding for the Willis'.

Sunlight socked him in the face and he paused to get his bearings. Voices rumbled from around the back of the barn.

I've got to move fast.

Mitch tucked Charles Law's knife in his belt loop, pushed off the barn door, and sprinted toward the distant woods. His legs, immobile for days, were wobbly. They shook as he fled around the house and through the bright open field behind the barn.

Faster!

"Hey! Haloo! There he is. Patty Cannon's boy!" The Constable's voice followed him as he ran away from the barn, and from the Willis family.

"Come on back here!" Joe Johnson joined in.

Faster. I've got to run faster.

"Come back here, you nigger!"

"You'll never get me!" Mitch panted out of earshot.

"Or, the Willis."

Chapter 27
Saturday Morning. Eavesdropping.

Ring.

Ring. Ring.

Mitch woke, tangled in his sweaty sheets. His whole body throbbed and his legs ached. He surveyed the room, then struggled to free himself. When he tossed the sheets aside, the peanuts Annie had given him and an old kitchen knife soared from the bed.

Mr. Law's knife!

Mitch patted the bed and his own body to make sure nothing else had traveled through his dream. Dumbstruck, he sat in the darkness of his bedroom and stared at the clock. The glow-in-the-dark numbers screamed, "2:45 AM."

Dear God, Patty Cannon is really messing with me.

A hint of light peeked under Mitch's door and he tiptoed toward it, making sure not to trip and alert his mom. "But Thomas, why your unit?" Mrs. Burke spoke on the phone in her bedroom. He opened his door a crack and listened.

"Well, the evening news didn't say which units. I just assumed the extension wouldn't include the reservists. You've been there for so long and you're supposed to be coming home this month. How much longer do they say?"

Dad's not coming home.

"I know. I know, I know, I know! A military wife is supposed to hang tough. But, I'm a *reservist's* wife! We don't have the same training!"

Mom's losing it.

Mitch heard nothing and assumed his Dad was now doing the talking.

"Thomas, I know. I just want you home. We all miss you and the kids need you. Annie is becoming very flippant and Mitchell is having an awful time of things."

Mitch strained to hear more.

"No. No, I think he just misses you." Mrs. Burke paused. "It's not like you to worry so much about him anymore. I just think he's feeling pressure from all sides. Swim team, school projects ..." Her voice trailed off.

Mitch opened his door an inch more, hoping to get better acoustics, but could hear nothing.

What's Dad saying?

His mom's voice picked up and he could hear her words again. "I will. I was planning on taking them out tomorrow—or, I guess it's today already. Anyway, I think we'll go to the pool."

I am so sick of the pool.

"Thomas, I just need you home." Her voice wavered. "I worry about you every minute."

She's crying.

The light from his mom's room clicked off and Mitch guessed it was some other soldier's turn to use the phone line. He shut the door, picked the peanuts and the knife up from the floor, and crawled back on the bed. He sat, with his back against the headboard, and watched the clock "2:59 A.M." He listened for his mom's voice.

Nothing.

He listened for any noise from Annie's room.

Nothing.

The stillness of the 3:00 A.M. bewitching hour gave Mitch room to think.

I need to be strong for Mom.

The glow-in-the dark numbers now read, "3:12 A.M."

I need to go back to sleep and deal with Patty Cannon. I need to settle this.

Mitch clutched the peanuts and knife in each hand and lay down on his side.

Dream. Plan. Work… work, work, work. And then, persist.

He curled his legs up to his chest and closed his eyes.

Dear God, believe it or not, I want to go back to sleep.

And he did.

Chapter 28

On to New Castle.

In broad daylight, Mitch burst onto the open field. The new shoes Mrs. Jenkins put on him squeezed his feet and slowed him down, making it difficult to put distance between him, Joe Johnson, and the barn. He almost scaled the barnyard fence when the angry Johnson gained on him, lunged at his legs, and tackled him to the ground.

"I got you, nigger boy!"

Mitch landed hard on his stomach, but was able to free himself of the man's clutches. "Stop using that word!" he screamed. He tripped forward as Johnson charged him.

The smell of stale whiskey oozed from Joe Johnson's pores and the man, still half drunk from the night before, tackled Mitch again, landing on his back. "You belong to the Missus and are comin' back with me!" Johnson slurred.

Mitch rolled from Johnson's hold and grabbed for the kitchen knife in his belt loop. Johnson scurried forward on his knees, but stopped when Mitch, leaning in a heap against the wooden fence, brandished the knife in front of him. "Leave me alone!" he yelled, scrambling back to his feet. "I don't belong to Patty Cannon!"

Followed by Charles, Constable Hardy huffed to the scene. "Hey. Hallo!" Seeing the knife in Mitch's hand, he drew his pistol to his side.

"That boy's dangerous!" Johnson wailed from the ground. "He done trying to kill a white man!" He stood and stumbled toward the Constable, creating an unfortunate vision of himself.

"Mr. Johnson," Constable Hardy barked, "I told you to keep away from the fugitive and leave the arresting to me." He pointed his gun at Johnson. "I don't trust the likes of you or any other of the Cannon woman's gang. Settle down!"

Mitch used both hands to point the knife at the men from his spot on the ground. "I don't belong to Patty Cannon. I'm free!"

"No, you ain't!"

"I said, hush, Mr. Johnson!"

Joe Johnson waived a dirty piece of paper above his head. "Says here this boy belongs to Missus Cannon!"

The Constable spat on the ground to his left and faced Charles. "Mr. Law, Johnson here has commitment papers on the boy."

Charles glanced over his shoulder at the barn in the distance, and then back at Mitch on the ground. He raised his hand to call for quiet. "Friend Hardy, this boy recently arrived from my cousin's home. Would thee take the word of Joe Johnson over the word of my own family relation?"

"That nigger ain't free!" Joe Johnson stabbed his finger at Mitch.

"Don't use that word!" Mitch glanced at his own arm, which had tanned his usual dark bronze over the summer.

The Constable stepped in his own spit and snatched the ownership papers from Joe Johnson, quickly reading the large type. "Mr. Law, these papers appear to be official." He faced Charles. "And, I've been given special direction by our local committees to track and capture all escaping fugitives."

Charles inhaled and folded his arms across his chest. "I understand thee is in an unkindly position. However, can thee be certain thy companion's paper is not a forgery?" He teetered on his black boot heels as he pointed to Johnson. "Perhaps, Friend Hardy, the Constable, we are in need of the Magistrate himself to assess the legal authenticity of the document."

A quiet rested on the group until the exasperated Constable spoke, waving his gun like a parade queen waves her hand. "Fine, sir. But, today is Sunday. We won't be finding the County Magistrate until tomorrow. Monday." He pursed his lips and squinted in the sun.

"I ain't waitin' 'til Monday," spat Johnson.

Mitch kept the knife pointed at Patty Cannon's son-in-law and remained leaning against the fence, occasionally bending his elbows to give his arms a rest.

"Ah, yes. Today is First Day. A quandary. What to do?" Charles rubbed his chin, tapped his temple, and then announced, "I believe the letter of the law does dictate the fugitive be removed to the nearest jail to overnight until the Magistrate arrives or has reviewed the documents." He finished his statement and smiled.

The words slowly resonated with Mitch. "Jail?" he shook his head. "I can't go to jail!"

Calmly, Charles said, "Son, thee has nothing to worry on. Thy papers will be verified as false in the morning."

Joe Johnson grumbled, "The nearest damn jail is over 20 miles north of here in New Castle!"

New Castle, Delaware? Historic New Castle?

"Sir," Constable Hardy dropped the gun to his side and addressed Charles. "Would you be willing to send us all by wagon?" He deliberated. "We'll drop the boy, fetch the Magistrate, and return your team by morning."

Charles kept his back to the barn and his eyes on the Constable. "Friend, I shall drive thee myself. As it were, I have some business to attend in New Castle."

Constable Hardy nodded and tucked his gun in his holster. "We will enjoy the company, Mr. Law."

Johnson pitched forward. "This ain't no party! I need to git this nigger boy back to the missus."

"Stop using that word!" Mitch yelled from the ground.

Nodding, Charles approached Mitch and stood over him. "The knife, son." He extended his hand and waited until Mitch pointed the blade to the ground, like he had been taught, and handed him his kitchen knife. Then, he took the knife in one hand and helped Mitch up with the other. As he did, he whispered in Mitch's ear, "Faith."

Charles hurried and, within minutes, drove from around the house a small covered black carriage led by two frisky grey mares. "I would like my charge upfront, with me if thee doesn't mind."

Constable Hardy handcuffed Mitch and helped him into the driving bench. "I've cuffed you in your front, as we have a long ride ahead. I trust you won't be pulling games on Mr. Law." Then, the Constable and Joe Johnson hoisted themselves up under the cream canopy of the carriage, Johnson struggling as he did and Charles quietly hurrying the process along.

He's trying to get them off the property before they see the Willis family, or Samuel. Wherever he is.

The carriage lurched off the property and turned onto the dusty road to New Castle. While Joe Johnson and Constable Hardy sat out of hearing range, Mitch suspected the less he talk to Charles Law, the better. Instead, he concentrated on the road before them and did not speak. Charles did the same. The sun labored from high in the sky and beat down on the stiff and hard driving bench.

Hours passed and the horses plodded on their course through cornfields and villages. In the village of Cantwell's Bridge, the carriage passed a white, simple building set back in a wooded grove, off the main road. A door swung opened on either side of the building, as if to balance the brick chimney that rose from the pitched roof. Charles slowed to a stop and waved to the women and men assembled at the doors.

"Hello, Friend!" His spirited voice rang clear as he waved, standing up from his seat.

Mitch sat up straight on the bench and buried his hands in his lap, conscious of the iron cuffs linking his wrists together. A white haired man smiled from the building steps, and nodded.

Mitch cleared his throat. "Is that your church?"

"We call that a Meeting House. I belong to another, but a Friend is welcome anywhere."

As the carriage moved forward, Mitch took his cues from Charles. Neither spoke, but remained focused on the journey. The two in the back must have been sleeping, for not a sound came from under the canopy as the carriage jostled along. Farms grew smaller as villages appeared to exist closer and closer together.

New Castle must be coming up.

The sun lowered and rested mid-sky above the tree line, dimming the daylight and painting a deep contrast between tree and sky. As if he read Mitch's mind, Charles said, "The city of New Castle approaches. Respite in even a jail sounds appealing about now!"

Mitch smiled faintly and the carriage continued, finally turning onto a wide cobblestone road. The sun quickened its exit and set below the horizon, but Mitch could still make out the city of New Castle before him. Dusty green lawns married with colonial brick buildings and walls to create a tidy, neat town, much like those he had read of in history books.

It looks pretty much like it does when I visited here with Dad ... except there are no cars or cafes.

"Hey ho, Mr. Law! Are we in New Castle, sir?" Constable Hardy yelled from his enclosed seat.

Charles leaned back in his bench towards the Constable's voice. "Yes, Friend. We are here."

"That nigger boy best be up front with ya, Mr. Law! No funny bizness."

"Hush, Johnson. Else, I will personally free the fugitive right here!" the Constable growled.

Charles smiled at the exchange and, for Mitch's benefit, pointed to one grand building that stood above the rest. "The courthouse and jail." He drove the party to the brick and marble building that served as courthouse, jail, Clerk's office, place of religious services, fancy balls, and dances. While pulling the horses to the post, Charles noted, "Fortune is on our side. The Sheriff's oil lamp appears to be lit. Perhaps he is in his quarters."

Mitch nodded agreement with Charles's assessment. At the same time, his stomach turned at the thought of sleeping in a jail. Marble steps greeted the carriage and a grand cupola atop the stately building looked down on the foursome. Charles climbed from the driver's bench to tie the horses to a post. The Constable and Joe Johnson tumbled from the carriage and landed on the steps next to Charles.

"Boy," the Constable addressed Mitch, "you'll step down with me now." He extended his arms to Mitch and helped him, still bound in handcuffs, jump from the bench and into the twilight.

Joe Johnson spat in the street. "Why you treatin' that nigger like he's somethin' special?" He wandered to the steps. "Let him git himself off the buggy."

DEAD: Joe Johnson, Ignorant, Drunk, Idiot, Age Unknown

Charles turned to the Constable. "Friend, as an authority, thee best knock on Friend Wilson, the sherriff's door. I believe it is to the side of the main building. I will await with my charge and the other, so it were." He pulled Mitch toward him by his shirtsleeve as the Constable nodded and approached the dark and quiet courthouse.

Minutes after the Constable explored the side entrance of the building, he appeared at the front steps and waved the trio over. Together, they walked along the side of the Courthouse to the door and, once inside that entrance, followed the Constable down a long corridor to the sheriff's office. The echoes of their footsteps announced their arrival to Sheriff Wilson, a stocky man with shaggy speckled hair and chin stubble that probably sprouted that evening. He sat sucking on a peach pit, his feet on a heavy wooden desk covered with papers. He squinted at his visitors as they entered the room.

"Evening, sirs." He addressed them all, but locked his pale blue eyes on Joe Johnson. "Ain't you been here before, sir?" He spat the slimy peach pit into his hand.

Charles smiled, the Constable shuffled his feet, Mitch coughed, and Joe Johnson stuttered, "I, I don't believe so." He fidgeted. "Lest not lately."

"Bullpucky." Sheriff Wilson stood erect behind the desk.

BUSTED: Joe Johnson, Stupid, Drunk, Idiot, Age Unknown

Standing, the sheriff reached Charles' shoulders. "Constable. Mr. Law. I've been working here, on the Lord's day of rest, all afternoon and all night and I'm getting right cranky. 'Sides that, my stomach ain't resting. State your business for me and make it fast, will you?"

Charles nodded politely and Constable Hardy spoke, tugging Mitch forward as he did so. "Sheriff Wilson, it seems we have a dispute over the ownership…"

Charles cleared his throat.

"The, um, ownership or *freedom* of this young man. Mr. Johnson here has presumed official papers stating ownership and Mr. Law has given his word that the boy is a distant relation."

Joe Johnson lurched forward and screamed, spit showering his audience, "He ain't no white relation! He's the property of the Missus Cannon!"

I am white. I'm actually white.

Sheriff Wilson stepped firmly forward and jerked the pistol from his holster. Thrusting it into Johnson's belly he said, "You show respect in this building and keep your trap shut, or you spend some more time behind the bars. This time, the key'll be tossed away!" Sheriff Wilson stared him down until he teetered backwards, behind the Constable. Mitch stepped closer to Charles, who didn't move.

Constable Hardy, his hat in one hand and papers in the other, shook his head. "So there, Sheriff. I got one party claiming ownership and the other claiming freedom. Seems proper to have the papers authenticated by the New Castle Magistrate." He stretched his arm out to present the papers to the sheriff.

Sheriff Wilson squinted as he read, turning the paper from one side to the other, looking for a clue to its authenticity. He spoke slowly. "I sure can't tell myself. There's a signature, but there ain't a Magistrate seal." He squinted his blue eyes again. "And gentlemen, I'm afraid to say, the New Castle Magistrate can't do you a spit of good." He looked up from his reading. "This document was drawn in Queen Anne's County. Only the Queen Anne's Magistrate can authenticate."

"What?!" Joe Johnson rattled his arms in the air.

Sheriff Wilson waived the paper and raised his voice. "What the hell did I tell you about keeping your trap shut?"

Charles intervened. "Friend Wilson, are you saying these gentlemen are in need of the seal from the Magistrate of Queen Anne's County in order to proceed with the confiscation of this boy?" He folded his arms across his chest.

"That's what I'm saying."

What are they saying?

Constable Hardy whistled, scratched his head, then spoke, "You mean to say that I need to take this lug of dirt and his papers all the way back to Queen Anne's … and then make the return trip once that Magistrate has sealed the papers?"

The sheriff nodded. "That's what I'm saying."

Joe Johnson shuffled and spit as he paced back and forth in the far corner of the room. Charles expressed little emotion, and held his chin in his hands. Constable Hardy grumbled, "You know, sometimes this honorable job just ain't worth the trouble." He began to pace on the opposite side of the room from Johnson.

Sheriff Wilson sat back down behind his desk. "Look. The boy can stay here for one night. But you best be coming back with the seal if you want to take him with you. Else, he goes free by Tuesday."

Free? From jail, or from Patty Cannon?

"Friend Hardy," Charles spoke up. "Thee best take my carriage and horses and be on thy way tonight. If thee departs now, thee will reach Queen Anne's by midnight and can be on the Magistrate's doorstep in the early morning. I am confident the Magistrate will come forth cooperatively at the prospect of ensuring the boy's freedom."

"And yourself, Mr. Law?"

"I have business I can tend to in New Castle tomorrow, the Second Day. I trust thee will retrieve the Magistrate's opinion and will hasten back to the jail to resolve this issue fairly. I will await thy return."

Why is he letting them do this?

"You have my word, Mr. Law."

"Hence thee have my wagon, Friend Hardy."

The sheriff escorted the party from his office, his pockets bulging and keys jangling from his belt. The Constable and Joe Johnson stumbled to the dark street where they stood arguing about finding a meal before their journey back. Charles spoke to the sheriff, with his eyes on Mitch. "Take care of my charge, Friend. And, we shall visit tomorrow." He exited.

"I take your word, Mr. Law. I always do." Sheriff Wilson closed the building's heavy door behind Charles and led Mitch further down the narrow hall, to the jail. He removed the handcuffs and opened the iron bar door to a small, dark, musty cell. Mitch entered the space and the bar door clanked shut behind him. Sheriff Wilson pulled a fresh peach from his breast pocket and handed it to Mitch through the bars. "Eat it up, then toss the pit to the hallway, else the rats'll come bothering you." He motioned down the forboding corridor. "You'll be better off if you toss aways."

"Yes, sir," Mitch spoke at last.

"Get your rest now. I suspect you might be needing it." The sheriff locked the cell door with one of his many keys and left Mitch by himself.

Mitch devoured the fuzzy peach and tossed the pit as far as he could through the bars. Next, he patted himself down for Annie's peanuts and Big Mo's jerky. He opened the peanut bag, guzzled them and the jerky down, licked the plastic bag, crushed it, said good-bye to Peanut Man, and tossed him after the pit.

Dear God. Anything but rats.

Chapter 29
Saturday Morning. To the Pool.

"Rise and shine, swimmer boy!" Mrs. Burke rested a tray on the dresser and opened the blinds in Mitch's room. The morning light exploded onto his face.

"No!" Mitch clutched the sheets over his face.

"Hey, you. It's me, Mom." She shook his shoulder. "Another nightmare?"

"What?" Mitch peeked out from the sheets. "Mom?" He looked around himself. "Oh, Mom!" He jumped out of bed, shook the sheets, and then patted the mattress.

"Mitchell, are you awake?" Mrs. Burke asked. "What are you doing?"

What happened to the peanut bag?

Mitch stood. "I'm looking for…um…I'm looking for the comic book I was reading last night." He stripped off the comforter and fell to his hands and knees to look underneath the bed.

Did it stay, or did it come back?

"Come on, honey. We're going out." She pointed to the tray on the dresser. "I brought you a bagel, juice and…get this… your morning obituaries."

The peanut bag stayed in the jail. It didn't come back with me.

Mitch surfaced at his mother's feet, snatched half a bagel, and took a huge bite, remembering the early morning phone call from his dad.

Mom looks tired. It's time to step up.

"Thanks." He glanced at the newspaper and then to his tired mother. With his mouth full of plain bagel, he said, "I think I'll pass on the paper today. Where are we going?"

"Pass on the obits? Heart be still." His mom yanked the paper from the tray. "We're going to the pool for the day. No arguing, okay?"

"I'm okay with going to the pool."

"Really?"

"Sure. Can we stop by the library?"

"Summer hours. It's closed today."

"Okay," Mitch readily agreed.

"Well, then. Your sister is waiting downstairs. Get your pool gear and meet us in the car." She rolled the newspaper and gently bopped Mitch on the head. "Thanks, hon." Mrs. Burke left the room and walked down the stairs.

Mitch tossed the bagel on the tray, rubbed his peach fuzzy chin, then raised both arms and inspected the new growth under his arm pits.

It's time, Mitchell Burke. You are in control. Shake Patty tonight. Swim the A meet tomorrow. Work it. Persist.

He brushed his teeth, packed his pool bag, and took the stairs two at a time to meet his mom and Annie at the minivan. Annie sat in the backseat, listening to a relaxation CD on Daryl's headset. Mitch settled into the front seat and the car pulled out of the narrow drive, on course to the pool. Random thoughts ping-ponged in his brain.

"Mom," he said after a few minutes, "I didn't hear Fritzi this morning. Do you think he came home to Petey?"

Annie coughed.

"I didn't hear the yapper, either. I don't know, Mitchell."

Annie coughed louder and silently kicked the back of Mitch's chair, extending her foot so he could feel the imprint of her big toe through the upholstery.

He turned in his seat to see Annie holding a note, which she lowered into her lap. Mitch read: "I heard Fritzi in my dream. Patty Cannon has the dog."

Mitch snapped back in his seat.

She took Fritzi.

They arrived at the community pool and parked under a shade tree. Mrs. Burke hurried ahead to capture deck chairs before the crowds came, but Mitch held Annie back by her arm. "I guess the comic books didn't work. You saw her, didn't you?"

Annie nodded. "I fell asleep before I could get to page two."

Mitch frowned and reached for the pool bags in the back of the van. "What do you mean you heard Fritzi?"

"Well, I was standing on the edge of Patty's meadow and I swear I heard him barking. You know, that obnoxious little yap."

"Did you see him?" he passed a loaded bag to Annie.

"No. And, I pretended I didn't hear him. I didn't want Patty to know I cared." She stared into the bag. "I thought you would like that."

Mitch shrugged. "Yeah, I guess."

"Why would she take Fritzi? I mean, he's not even your dog or anything."

"I think she's just trying to mess with my head." He closed the trunk, leaned against the blue van, and bounced the pool bag against his knees. "I think she's showing me she can move in and out of my world, and take what she wants."

Annie stiffened. "She might be able to get the dumb dog, but she can't have me."

"Yeah, and we have to keep it that way." He pushed off the car. "What about Josiah? Did you see him this time?"

"No. Patty said he wasn't feeling well so he couldn't come out to play."

"She's still playing games with you? That's good, I think."

"I told you, Mitch. She's nice to me. She just talks nice and plays games. Of course, she always asks about you, but I don't tell her anything."

"Keep it that way. Okay?"

"You've got my word."

Annie and Mitch walked through the pool house to the deck, where their mother had arranged three lounge chairs sitting in a row.

"Oh my God. She's sitting with Daryl," Mitch hissed as they approached her.

"Lord's name. In vain. Again."

"Give me a break."

"Look who I found!" Mrs. Burke announced when she saw her children.

Daryl stood from the chair and extended his hand out and onto Mitch's shoulder. "Hey, Dude. What's up?"

"Nothing. I mean, nothing much. I mean, my mom wanted to come here today..."

"Hey, look. I know what you're thinking." Daryl said. "You're thinking I'm going to talk about tomorrow's swim meet."

"Ugh," Mitch moaned.

"But I'm not."

"Really?"

"Sure. You already know what to do in the pool tomorrow."

"Uh, okay."

"So, your mom tells me you're working on a history project. What's it about?"

Mitch eyed Daryl with suspicion. "Do you really want to know?"

"Heck, yeah! I'm on a history scholarship at the university. I can never get enough of the stuff."

"I thought you liked to swim."

Daryl chuckled. "I swim because I love it. But, I *inhale* history. Tell me about your project."

As Mrs. Burke and Annie settled into the lounge chairs with their magazines, Mitch fumbled through a description of his imaginary report on the Underground Railroad, making sure to avoid mention of Patty Cannon.

Daryl listened to every word and offered bits of advice. "Just remember, the Underground Railroad is one of the coolest movements this country has ever seen."

"What do you mean, 'cool?'" Mitch asked. "I mean, what would make slaves running for their lives 'cool?'"

Daryl, sounding more like a scholar than a swim coach, faced Mitch. "Look at it this way, since it involved so many different types of people, fighting for their liberties, some historians consider it to be the first civil rights movement in the United States. And, talk about Winning Plans! These people *invented* Dream, Plan, Work, Persist!"

Mitch absorbed Daryl's words as he watched two boys dive into the shallow end of the pool. The lifeguard's whistle blew and the boys were sent to the deep end. Finally, Mitch scrunched his face and risked a thought. "You mean, Harriet Tubman was a civil rights activist?"

"Yo, baby!" Daryl high-fived Mitch. "You totally get it!"

"Thanks." Mitch said. "I just think she's *cool*."

They both laughed and Daryl punched his shoulder. "Gotta run."

Mitch spent his day at the pool swimming laps and obsessing. His thoughts darted from the New Castle jail, to Patty and the Johnson Gang, to Josiah, to Daryl, to his mom, to his dad, and to Annie.

What a mess.

And then he thought about Fritzi.

If she can get Fritzi, will she finally get Annie? What about Josiah? What will she do to Josiah?

He worried all day—through his laps, through lunch, and on the ride back home in the van. He worried until the van pulled into the driveway and his mom barked orders. "Let's go guys, we've got a few hours before Mass. Annie, please clean your room."

"Mass?" Annie whined. "Why do we have to go to church tonight?"

"Mitch is swimming the A meet tomorrow morning, so we'll be going to Saturday evening Mass. Tonight."

Mitch dropped his head back on the headrest.

I wish she didn't bring up the A Meet.

"Besides," she spoke, "tonight is spaghetti and bingo night. It'll be fun."

"I *hate* the spaghetti those old ladies make!" Annie yelled.

Mrs. Burke twirled in her seat to face her daughter. "End of story, Anna Maria."

Mitch poked his sister from behind. "Pull it together and don't give Mom a bad time."

"Okay." Annie sighed. "*Sarge.*" She slid from the van and into the house.

Mitch opened the door and swung out his legs. "I think I'm going to take a nap."

I'm going to break out. I'll get to Canada and break free.

"Fine by me. Get your rest for tomorrow." Mrs. Burke had exited the van and unlocked the house door. "I'll wake you for Mass."

Once in the house, Mitch went down to the dark basement, dug through his father's metal tool chest, retrieved a small hacksaw and hid it under his shirt. Then, he walked the two flights of stairs to his bedroom. He shut the door, lay on his back on the twin bed with the hacksaw by his side, and closed his eyes. His right hand clutched the saw.

Come and get me. I'm ready.

Mitch eyed the white stucco ceiling above him and counted the plaster bubbles in the paint. He closed his eyes at 128, but continued counting in his head. At 345, he became drowsy, and at 476, he fell asleep.

Chapter 30

A Wakeup Call.

Mitchell Thomas Burke opened his eyes in the complete blackness of the jail cell. He could see nothing. He felt the cool, damp dirt floor for the hacksaw and found it at his side.

I did it!

He grabbed the saw and scrambled to his feet, patting the cold and damp brick walls for support. The cell was small, boxed in by three walls and an iron bar door facing a stone corridor. He patted the walls and the floor until he felt the coolness of iron, and then stroked the bars with his free hand.

I can cut these. I know I can.

Mitch rested the hacksaw on the floor and ran both hands over the uneven bars, searching for weak spots or divots in the iron. His eyes slowly adjusted to the lack of light and he could see his hands before him. His fingernails were dirty and his skin rough, darkened, and worn.

They don't look like my hands.

He brought one hand closer to his eyes and studied it.

Sometimes, I don't feel like I'm me.

Mitch placed his hand back on the bar and refocused his attention. He had cut metal before, with his dad.

The job will be easier if I start at a weak joint.

When he found a suitable starting spot, he picked the hacksaw back up and quietly laid the tiny teeth of the blade to the bar.

Hopefully, the sheriff went home for the night.

Slowly, he moved the blade forward and away from him.

"Mitchell! Mitchell Burke!"

Mitch recoiled from the bars, his heart leaping from his chest. He dropped the hacksaw to the ground and immediately picked it back up. He retreated to the brick corner of the cell and caught his breath before he spoke.

"Mom? Mom, is that you?"

Chapter 31

Saturday Evening. To Church.

"Mitchell, you have got to wake up. We're going to be late for church." Mrs. Burke stood over Mitch as he lay in the fetal position, hugging the hacksaw to his chest.

"Mom?" He rolled onto his back. "Mom? What are you doing here?" He looked up at the familiar plaster bubbles on the ceiling.

"What am I doing here? I've been calling you for ten minutes. What are you doing with Dad's saw in your bed?"

Oh, God.

Mitch shot out of bed, brushed past his mother, and put the hacksaw on his dresser. "I, um...borrowed it for my project and must've left it on the bed by mistake." He ran his nervous fingers through his tussled hair.

I brought it back.

"You're lucky you didn't cut yourself."

"I know."

"Well, we've got to hurry. Father Bob called and asked if Annie could fill in as an altar server. The Beckman boy is sick." She turned to go.

"Mom?" Mitch hesitated. "Do you ever feel, you know, sometimes 'not white?'"

His mom raised her right eyebrow and scrutinized her son. "You've been dreaming. Why don't you splash some water on your face and meet me in the car in five minutes?" Before Mitch could answer, his mom was out the door.

Whoa.

Mitch turned to the saw and ran a finger along the blade, which was warm to the touch.

Double whoa.

The three rode to church in silence, except for the occasional sigh from Annie. Once in the parking lot, Mrs. Burke said, "Chin up, Anna Maria. No one's life ever ended because she had to serve an extra Mass in the month." She moved Annie's hair from her face. "Run, or you'll be the late altar server."

Annie rolled her eyes and set off in a jog for the side door of the red brick church. Mitch and his mom ambled on the stone path, around the statue of

Mary, to the carved wooden front door. Here, the summer church crowd—post-pool and pre-Saturday night barbecue—was entering. Mrs. Burke briefly greeted a few ladies before leading Mitch down the blue carpeted center aisle, to the very front pew. There, he closed his eyes and sank to his knees to say a quick prayer before Mass started.

Please God, don't let Mrs. Cruz ask me to bring up the wine and host today.

Almost on cue, the short Mrs. Cruz appeared from the side aisle, stoically marched in front of the empty altar, genuflected, turned to the center aisle, and launched her search for the evening's gift bearer.

Mitch dove into the pew, as if looking for something that dropped from his pocket. His mother, eyes closed in prayer, didn't notice. But stately Mrs. Watson, moving into the seat next to Mitch, did.

"Dear, can I help you find something?" Her rich voice carried as she squeezed in next to the Burkes.

"No, ma'am." She was loud, but Mitch had always liked Mrs. Watson. She was his savior from boredom at the church spaghetti dinners, spinning purple and gold tales about her royal African ancestors. Perhaps the stories were true, or perhaps they weren't. But, no matter the story, Mrs. Watson always finished her telling with a generous laugh.

Seeing that Mrs. Cruz passed his pew, Mitch scrambled to take his seat under the slow effort of the overhead ceiling fans.

Thank you, God.

His mother finished her prayers, smiled, nodded at Mrs. Watson, and peacefully sat back from the kneelers. As she did, organ music wafted from the choir loft and the priest and company entered the church and took their places on the altar. Mass began.

Mrs. Cruz read the First Reading, from the Book of the Prophet Isaiah, while Father Bob, the two altar servers, and the congregation looked on. Father Bob was short on summer volunteers, so Mrs. Cruz also read the Second Reading, from the Letter to the Hebrews. Mitch tried to follow, but gave up when she came to pronounce the Hebrew names. Her thick Spanish accent couldn't navigate the "h"s and "j"s of Hebrew, rendering the weighty sentences containing the names Tarshish, Mosoch, and Javan impossible to follow. Instead, Mitch diverted his attention to his sister.

What'll she do today?

Usually, the blond-haired Annie looked like an angel when sitting on the altar in her white frock. Mitch knew better, of course. His mother had worked hard with Annie for the past year to improve her "altar etiquette." If a member of the congregation were to watch carefully, he might see Annie chewing gum, yawning without covering her mouth, or flashing the peace sign from under her robes to anyone sitting in the front pew. To anyone, that is, but her mother.

This evening, Annie appeared quiet and resigned to her position as a devout altar server. When the congregation stood to listen to Father Bob read the Gospel, Mitch turned his attention to Mrs. Watson, who had just belted out, "And also with you." He leaned on the pew back in front of him, resting his hand right next to her large left hand.

She is so dark and I am so white.

He concentrated on the difference in skin tone until Father Bob finished reading. The congregation and the altar servers sat to listen to Father's Homily. Mitch studied his own hands as they sat in his lap.

I'm not even close to being black.

Father spoke about compassion and honesty. "Compassion," he said, "is not a trait owned by any race, creed, or sex. We are all put here to feel compassion, and to act on it."

Mitch kept one ear on the sermon, and his eyes on Annie. She sat behind Father Bob, her eyes on the tiled altar floor, and not on the lecturing priest.

What's she thinking?

Her head tilted a bit forward and her shoulders were now slouching forward as well. Next, her body jerked an inch or so to the right side arm of her chair.

She's falling asleep!

His sister pulled out of the first signs of slumber and sat back erectly into her cushioned seat. Within a minute, her shoulders slumped again and her eyes rolled shut. Mitch looked at his mom, who wasn't watching Annie, and then looked back at his sister whose chin was now touching her chest. Slowly, her head rolled to one side.

She can't fall asleep. Not here. Not before she reads the comics!

Mitch sat forward in the pew and coughed into his hand as loudly as he could. His mother frowned at him. A startled Annie flashed her eyes open. She shook her head to clear it. Mrs. Burke focused on the sermon, Mitch glared at Annie, and Mrs. Watson now cleared her throat.

Father's sermon continued. "Honesty we owe first to ourselves. When we're honest with ourselves, we can then pass the honesty on to our surrounding relationships."

Annie looked down from the altar and mouthed, "What?"

Mitch looked to either side of Father Bob as spoke and then, in return, mouthed, "DON'T fall asleep!"

Mrs. Burke kept her eyes on the priest, but Mrs. Watson kept her eyes on

Mitch. He, in turn, bored holes into his sister with his stare.

Annie nodded at Mitch and then casually browsed the altar as Father Bob spoke. "Your word. Your word is you. Live by your word and you will find peace."

As her eyes focused on her feet, Annie's chin coasted to her chest.

She's falling asleep again!

"Think your words through before you promise, and your promises will always be deliverable."

I promised her Patty wouldn't get her.

Mitch leaned even further over the pew back. "Psst!"

Mrs. Watson didn't waste a minute. She stood up, right there in the front pew, puffed out her huge bossom and bellowed, "Wake up, Annie Burke!"

Annie snapped awake, Mrs. Burke covered her open mouth, Mitch sat square in his seat, and Father Bob stopped his sermon. He turned to face Annie and said, "Dear child, am I putting you to sleep?"

Mitch smiled.

She won't fall asleep now.

The congregation roared with laughter and Annie put both hands over her face. From her spot in the pew, Mrs. Watson called, "Don't worry, Annie. I just didn't want you falling off your chair. You may continue, Father."

"Thank you, Mrs. Watson." Father Bob picked up the pace, closed his sermon, led the congregation in the sign of the peace and communion, and brought the service to a merciful end. For the first time Mitch could ever recall, the Burke family was the first to leave the church after Mass, skipping spaghetti bingo.

Chapter 32

Saturday Evening. To Bed.

"I still can't believe you had Mrs. Watson shout at me like that." Annie lay on the bottom bunk, her feet pressing up on the bed above her. Mitch sat at her desk wearing striped boxers and a "Fear the Bug" team T-shirt, writing on a pad of lined paper.

"I told you. I didn't ask Mrs. Watson to do that. And besides, she helped you. You cannot go to sleep without me, Annie. You need me."

"If she were such a help, maybe Mom wouldn't have pulled my ear for falling asleep on the altar." She punctuated her words with kicks to the mattress above her.

"Pull it together." He ripped a sheet from the pad and moved the chair to the side of Annie's bed. "Look, I wrote out a list of the best *Cosmic Comic*s to read, in chronological order." He handed the list to Annie, along with a stack of 15 comic books.

She sat up to receive the stash. "You're really going to let me read all of these?"

"Only if you read the stories I listed first. If you read these, then I'll give you more."

"Thanks, bro!" Annie stacked the books by her pillow and opened the first to read.

"If you do see Patty tonight, remember don't tell her anything about me and don't let her know you know what she's up to."

Annie nodded, "Okay. But you need to remember Daryl's Winning Plan." She stuck her nose in *Cosmic Comic* 114, the first on Mitch's list.

Mitch smiled. "Okay. Goodnight then." Having already said goodnight to his mother, he retreated to his own room. He removed the old hacksaw from his bureau and buried it under his covers. He then grabbed the *National Geographic* magazine and his notes from under his bed and settled down next to the hacksaw.

Maybe I've missed something in here.

Mitch opened the magazine to the first page of the article. He whispered, "Escape from Slavery, The Underground Railroad." On the opposite page, a young Harriet Tubman greeted his eyes. In the picture, a black and white photo of the serious woman rested atop a bible. On the bible sat a burning candle inside a white teacup. Mitch read the worn margin:

"Moses to her people, Harriet Tubman was born a slave in Maryland and as a young woman fled north to freedom in 1849. There, she joined and inspired the Underground Railroad, a vast informal network of activists—black and white—who aided escaping slaves in the decades before the Civil war. Though she could not read, she knew her Bible and felt no fear, because, she told fellow conductor Thomas Garrett, she 'ventured only where God sent.'"

Hmm. Father Bob and Mom would like that. Too bad she can't help me.

Mitch flipped from Harriet Tubman, to the "Flight to Freedom, United States 1860" map; the map that he desperately wanted to point him to freedom. He followed the swirl of the orange arrows from south to north, looking for details that weren't there. His left hand on the hacksaw, his right forefinger traced the arrows as Annie's words and Daryl's Winning Plan popped back into his head.

Dream…Plan…Work…Persist

Over and over again he traced—trancelike—until he fell into a profound sleep.

Chapter 33

Thomas Garrett.

Mitch woke in the corner of his cell, sitting scrunched over his hacksaw. Morning light flooded the hallway outside the black den, illuminating his castaway peanut bag and peach pit. Voices echoed from down the hall.

"I am pleased to be in thy company as well, Friend Wilson."

Mitch heard a clear, but unfamiliar voice from the sheriff's office. He stood, fumbling the hacksaw.

Oh, my God. What do I do with this?

"And Charles," Sheriff Wilson said, "I do believe you have friends in all of the proper places."

Where can I put it?

Mitch propped his father's hacksaw in the shadowed corner of the bare cell and approached the bars to better hear the men's conversation. His nerves settled when he heard the familiar chortle of Charles Law, followed by his voice. "Friend Wilson, Friend Garrett here is a friend to us all, as thee understands better than most in the county."

Garrett? Does he mean Thomas Garrett? Thomas Garrett, friend-of-Harriet-Tubman Thomas Garrett?

"And Friend Wilson, sheriff."

Is that Thomas Garrett speaking?

"As customary, we appreciate thy consideration in the matters at hand."

"Thomas," replied the sheriff …

It is Thomas Garrett!

"I'm just tending to my job. You brought me here a release signed by Chief Justice Booth. How you're able to snitch a judge's signature before the sun come up is beyond me, but it ain't my job to question the Chief Justice." Sheriff Wilson coughed. "It says here I can in no way keep this boy if there ain't no evidence to hold him. 'In the absence of evidence,' it says here, 'the presumption is always in favor of freedom.'"

Mitch strained to hear, but couldn't. Finally, Charles spoke loud and clear. "Therefore, the fraudulent commitment papers on the boy hold no more weight than my word he is a free nephew of my cousin."

"But alas Friend," Thomas Garrett said, "thy word carries more than just weight, as it leans in the likely direction of the presumption of freedom."

What are they saying?

"Yep," said the sheriff. "The boy is free and if I were you, gentlemen, I'd have him outta that cell before another bird wakes. Lord only knows how quickly that Johnson jackass can ride the Constable back here with more questionable papers."

I'm free?!

"Friend Wilson, my carriage awaits transport to Wilmington," Garrett said.

"And I will await the return of Friend Hardy, his Johnson charge, and my carriage," Charles added.

"Damn if that won't be a scene. Happy to have you at my side for that one. I'm getting too old for this crap."

Keys jangled, followed by the men's footsteps. Mitch stepped back from the bars when the three men approached his cell, apparently not noticing the peanut bag in the hallway. Sheriff Wilson spoke as he unlocked the bar door. "Morning, son. I suspect your ears have been to the bars, but just in case they haven't, you're free to go with Mr. Garrett here."

A sandy-haired man about 30 years old turned his grey eyes and wide pale face to Mitch. Thomas Garrett smiled and extended his hand. Mitch shook the strong hand and stepped out of the cell.

He's a lot younger than in the National Geographic *picture.*

"I suggest you beat your trail right away." The sheriff closed the door behind Mitch and the four headed in silence to the front door of the jail. "Pleasure doing business with you, gentlemen." He opened the door and Mitch stepped outside into the sultry morning with Thomas Garrett and Charles Law. He squinted through streaks of sunlight to see a carriage tethered behind two dark horses positioned alongside the three-foot-high upping block.

I'm standing with Thomas Garrett!

"Friend Wilson," Charles said, "I will be taking a meal at the Van Dyke residence. Can I impose upon thee to send word when Friend Hardy and Joe Johnson arrive in New Castle?"

"I'll send word as soon as their heels hit these steps. The less time that Johnson scoundrel spends in my building, the better." He extracted a fuzzy fruit from his pocket. "Any of you like a peach?"

Thomas Garrett led Mitch down the stairs by his elbow, "No sir. But, we thank thee for thy compassion and trust we will meet again in the near future."

"Blasted, I'm sure you will." Sheriff Wilson gave a quick wave from inside the building and slammed the imposing door to the jailhouse.

The two men and Mitch stood by the clean black carriage. "Friend," Thomas Garrett addressed Charles Law. "Thee has once again shone like a prince. Humanity is grateful."

Charles smiled and rested his hand on Mitch's shoulder. "I am happy to have been of service to thee, and now, thee is in the best of care, son. Farewell." Charles stepped onto Market Street.

Thomas Garrett nodded to Charles, climbed the steps of the wooden upping block, and into the driver's seat of the carriage. Mitch stood in the street, watching Charles Law walk away. "Um. Um." Finally, he shouted, "Thank you very much, sir!"

Charles turned, waved at Mitch, and continued on his way.

"Come now, child. We have a distance to cover before the return of the intoxicated Joe Johnson and Friend Hardy." Thomas Garrett patted the bench beside him.

Mitch walked in front of the horse to the opposite side of the carriage. Before ascending he asked, "Don't you want to handcuff me?"

"Today thee rides as the nephew to the cousin of Friend Charles Law. Come aboard."

Wow.

As the upping block sat only on the driver's side of the carriage, Mitch pulled himself up the three feet, and into the passenger seat, next to a wide wicker basket. Thomas Garrett jerked the reins and moved the carriage away from the jail steps. Immediately, they passed a large brick building flanked by cannons along its exterior sidewalls.

That's the old arsenal. I remember it on the tour with Dad.

Next, the carriage plodded past a large brick structure surrounded by a cemetery.

And that's Immanuel Church.

Thomas Garrett interrupted Mitch's thoughts. "The distance to travel is long." He nodded toward the basket. "My Margaret set forth a fine meal for thy enjoyment. I suggest thee eat and rest whilst I navigate our way."

Mitch needed no encouragement and peeled the yellow cloth off the basket. From it, he removed biscuits smelling of bacon and, to his stomach's delight, sweet, moist, golden cornbread. At the bottom of the basket, he found fresh peaches and smiled. As the carriage passed through the waking streets of New Castle and onto a dirt road, which led them along the Christina River and out of town, he nervously sucked on the first juicy peach that met his fingers.

The road forked to the west, away from the river. The stoic Thomas Garrett gave the horses little, if any direction. They knew the way. From his perch, Mitch watched one red barn, and then the next, appear a mile or so apart off the roadway. At least an hour passed before he found the courage to address the historic figure.

"Sir?"

Thomas Garrett glanced to the right. "Thee speaks!" His gentle grin canvassed the width of his face.

"Sir, why do you do it?"

"I was told thee is a lad of few words, yet I now understand thee saves thy words for important matter." Thomas Garrett raised his bushy eyebrows. "Why does thee ask?" He encouraged the horses along with a flick of the reins. "Should not man help man? Is that not a human ambition?"

Mitch shifted in his seat. "But, you...you and the others...you risk your lives...for people you don't know."

"Life is relative to thy condition, is it not? There is not one life—known or unknown by me—that is less important than my own."

"I don't get it."

Thomas Garrett let some time pass before he spoke to Mitch. "Son, when I rest my head to sleep at night, I have the privilege of dreaming about the best of my day. I see the harvest, and my lovely Margaret, and my small children... all there to comfort me." The horses plodded through the heat. "And what is it that thee dreams about?"

Mitch pulled in his stomach and rubbed his neck. "Um...well, I dream about her. I dream about Patty Cannon."

Thomas Garrett nodded and again let minutes pass before he spoke. "And the other enslaved peoples, they too dream of the worst of their day. They dream of their sad reality. We are born of the same maker, yet while most of us are allowed peace in our dreams, there are others that can not rest even then."

Mitch watched small stones sputter from the carriage wheels as they passed on the dirt road.

"The villains of slavery have taken away the human right to peace of dream."

Mitch rubbed the palms of his hands down his thighs. "You're right. They steal your dreams."

The pair rode for another full hour before Mitch spoke. "What made you start?"

"Start?" Thomas Garrett scratched his head. "I do not recall a 'start' per se. But, I will tell thee I gave my word when a free family friend was kidnapped to sell south. The day I won her freedom, I gave my word that I would assist the needy that crossed my doorstep."

"Who did you give your word to?"

"To myself, son!" Thomas Garrett blurted. "Thy word to thyself is a gift from God. Speak the truth and have the courage to honor thy own word."

"Father Bob says, 'Your word is you. Live by your word and you will find peace.'"

"Where is thy father, son?"

Mitch placed his hands on the bench at either side of him. "He's not my father. I mean, I'm talking about our priest. My father is...gone." He turned his head away from Thomas Garrett and watched the Delaware landscape jostle by. The countryside had changed along the ride and the neat rows of corn that Mitch was used to seeing now scaled rolling hills.

Thomas Garrett puffed up his chest and let out a huge sigh. "But of course. I tell thee son, stand firm in the faith and thee will meet thy father in the spirit."

"But..."

He patted Mitch's knee. "Be a man of courage."

"But...my father's not d—"

"Look ahead, son. Look at thy land of freedom!" Thomas Garrett pulled the horses and carriage to a stop at a dusty crossroad. He thrust out his thick arm and pointed ahead of him.

Mitch dropped the conversation about his father and looked off to the distance. "Where are we?"

"We are on the line between the states of Delaware and Pennsylvania." Thomas Garrett stiffened his shoulders and whispered. "Hear me. Today it is not wise for me to transport thee directly into Kennett Square. Rather, I will have thee descend at this border and thee will walk of thy own accord into freedom."

A single white stone marker, about two feet high, jutted from the roadside, the Letter "P" for Pennsylvania carved on its top.

"Freedom?" The word fell from Mitch's mouth.

"Freedom awaits."

"So easy? I just walk over the line?"

"I can only assume 'easy' is not a word used by thy supporters."

Josiah. Wilson Lee. Mary. The Rosses. Big Mo. Samuel Burns. Mrs. Jenkins. Charles Law. They sacrificed so much.

Mitch's heart beat faster. "No, it hasn't been easy."

"True freedom never is."

Chapter 34

It's Her.

"Now, thee needs to walk on this road that belongs to Pennsylvania and step quickly until thee comes to a stone gate post." Thomas Garrett carefully articulated his instructions. "Then, turn in. I have sent word in advance to the Agnew family. Those kind Friends will provide lodging and work whilst thee settles."

"Settle? In Pennsylvania?"

Thomas Garrett nodded. "I, in the by and by, will return to Wilmington, where I am sure to defend myself against the Johnson gang slurs and accusations." He snickered. "But, thee as my witness, I am not transporting thee across the state line, am I? Thee is bringing thyself to freedom."

"But, how can I be free in Pennsylvania?" Mitch jiggled in his seat as he looked down on his road to supposed freedom.

"By its own laws, Pennsylvania has been a free state since 1780, son."

"I thought slaves ran all the way to Canada. Shouldn't I go to Canada?"

Thomas Garrett held the reins close to his stomach and leaned closer to Mitch. "Perhaps thee has foresight. If another Fugitive Slave Act is passed, I can see the need for the poor souls to leave this country entirely." He sat back in his seat. "In the meantime, I suggest thee get onto free soil before a bounty hunter comes our way. Rest and recover with the Agnew family before thee makes any decision to move on." He pointed to the road.

Mitch slowly stood in the carriage, his knees wobbling under his weight.

"Go on now. I would like to watch as freedom sinks into thy heels."

Dream. Plan. Work.

Mitch inhaled for strength before jumping onto the hard dirt road. He walked in front of the carriage, approached the "P" state line marker, and took one step beyond it, into Pennsylvania. He stroked the smooth marker and looked down at his hands. They tingled at first, and then started to visibly shake.

"What's happening?"

Mitch looked up to see Thomas Garrett waving at him, from the carriage in Delaware. "Those are the hands of a free man!" The Quaker yelled as he directed the sweaty horses to turn around and pull the carriage away.

Mitch looked back down at his shaking hands. The shakes rose from his once smooth, clean, swimmer hands, through his arms, into his torso, and down his legs. His entire body shook. Even his head shook as if he were still riding on the carriage that now faded as it rolled away. Mitch's shakes swelled through his body and slowly ended, but the tingle remained and he now wore his striped boxers and team T-shirt instead of the 19th century clothes he became accustomed to.

It worked. Daryl's Winning Plan worked!

Mitch placed both hands on his head and inhaled deeply. He was beginning to feel composed when he heard a familiar, annoying, noise.

Is that a bark?

He looked back at his tingling hands and then up at the road.

Fritzi!

There, in the spot where Thomas Garrett's carriage had been, sat Petey's dog, his tail wagging so hard it shook his entire body.

"Fritzi, it's you!" Mitch ran on free soil to the Delaware line. Fritzi stood on his four short legs and barked like a mastiff. "Come on boy. Let me take you back to Petey." Mitch leaned over the state line to pick up the feisty little dog.

Suddenly, Fritzi's tail stopped wagging, and instead curled between his hind legs, and he barked again. Louder.

"It's okay, boy." Mitch reached for the dog.

Swish!

Patty Cannon, her black hair wildly circling her face, lunged from behind a thorny bush. "Likely it's alright for you...but not for me!" Blood from thorn punctures bubbled like bursting berries on her muscled forearms.

"Patty!" Mitch grabbed the dog and fell backwards, with Fritzi on his belly, onto the Pennsylvania road. "Go away. Leave me alone! I'm...I'm free!"

"Boy, you've got some learning to do." A red-faced Patty screamed from the Delaware line. "You aren't free 'til I set you free!"

Mitch stumbled to his feet, clutching the dog to his chest.

Persist.

"That's not true. Thomas Garrett told me I'm free!"

Patty spat over the line and onto the Pennsylvania Road. "Thomas Garrett!" She licked her full, cracked lips, slid her hair behind her ears, and whispered, "Mitchey-boy, why would you want to leave me and Josiah, now? We were having so much fun together. Just like a proper family."

"You're not my family!"

"Well, now." She rubbed her hands on her dirty skirt. "Josiah considers you kin."

"He hates you!" Mitch stepped backwards with Fritzi. "He would leave you if he could."

"He's mine!" She raised a tight fist in the air.

"You kidnapped him!" Fritzi wriggled in his arms as Mitch looked over his shoulder at the long, dusty road to the Agnew farm.

Should I just go? Will she follow me?

He took one step backward, deeper into Pennsylvania.

Persist.

Patty darted ten yards down the Delaware line and roared, "Josiah belongs to me!" She thumped her thumb against her full chest. "He belongs to me!"

"He does not." Mitch took another step backward.

She's not coming closer.

"Josiah belongs to me, and so do you!" She ran the ten yards back to her starting point. "You owe me. Your family owes me!"

"We don't owe you anything!" Mitch shouted as Fritzi squirmed.

"My pappy died because of your kin!"

"He was a murderer!" Mitch watched her scurry ten yards in the other direction, following the state line.

She can't cross the state line.

"Your kin are so righteous. So full of God that my pappy went hanging from a tree! You will suffer regret for this!"

I think I'm really free.

"Josiah is mine!" Patty screamed as Mitch put distance between them. "Josiah is mine!"

Mitch held Fritzi tight, turned and rushed for the Agnew Farm. He ran and didn't look back.

I'm free. She can't get me.

Mitch ran until the screaming from the state line grew distant and faint.

"I know where your sister dreams!"

Mitch ran towards the farm.

I already know that.

He clutched the squirming dog.

I know that. But you don't know that I know that.

Chapter 35

Sunday Morning.

"Fritzi, knock it off." A groggy Mitch pushed the squirming dog off his chest and away from his face. "Stop licking me."

Mitch sat up, and the dachshund tumbled off the bed. "What? We're home?"

Fritzi barked from the floor.

"Shh!" Mitch tossed his pillow at the dog. "Shut up! I mean, don't bark!" He lept from the bed and swept Fritzi into his arms, looked out his bedroom window at the sun rising in the east, then back into his room, at the digital clock. "Five thirty three." He rubbed the dog's head, sending its tail to wag furiously. "We made it out Fritzi, we made it out."

The dog barked again.

"Shh!" Mitch desperately cupped his hand over Fritzi's moist pointed snout, tucked him under his left armpit, and opened the bedroom door with his right hand. "I gotta get you outta here." He snuck into the hallway and tiptoed past his mother's room...

No lights on.

...and then past Annie's room.

No noise.

Mitch snuck past the bedrooms, down the stairs, and outside without waking his mother or sister. When he stepped onto the warm driveway he took a deep breath and exhaled, "Okay Fritzi, time for you to go home to Petey." Mitch walked across the damp lawn to the Kimmel's house and gently sat Fritzi on the front step, patting his head as he released him on the rubber door mat. On his own turf, the dog barked, and Mitch jogged back to his own home.

The morning sky opened like a canvas of color. Mitch enjoyed the familiar oranges and purples ripple above him while he rubbed the grass off his bare feet before entering the house.

"What are you doing, Mitch?" Annie popped from behind the door.

"Argh!" He gasped.

"It's just me."

"Annie, you scared me!" He caught his breath. "What are you doing up?"

"I heard barking." She leaned forward and whispered, "You got him, didn't you? You brought Fritzi back."

Mitch moved his sister aside and entered the house, peeking around the corner of the mud room. "Is Mom still asleep?"

Annie nodded.

"I think I'm free. I'm not sure, but I think I got rid of Patty Cannon forever."

Annie whisked her hands to her hips and said, "Of course you're free. I could've told you that. But, did you get Fritzi?"

"Yeah. He's home. What do you mean 'of course I'm free'?"

"Patty's zipped from nice to hot as all get out. Man, you should've heard her swear when you crossed into Pennsylvania. She told us all about it. She even told me I had to go."

"What?!"

Annie walked into the kitchen. "Just that. She said, 'Girl, you've got to go for now. I need to speak to Josiah in private.'"

Mitch followed and sat at the counter. "You're kidding."

"Nope. Not kidding." She opened the refrigerator and started her morning breakfast expedition.

"Annie," Mitch spoke slowly, "What about Josiah? How was he?"

"Ooh," she extracted a gallon of orange juice and closed the refrigerator. "Not good, bro. He looked like he was going to get sick or something. And I think he might've been crying." Annie paused. "But, Patty said not to worry, that she would take care of him."

Mitch swallowed. "Take care of him?"

"Mom! What are you doing up?" Annie blurted over Mitch's shoulder.

She's going to hurt Josiah.

Mitch turned around to see his mother, dressed in shorts, flip-flops, and his dad's Navy T-shirt, entering the kitchen behind him. "That darn dog must be back. Did you hear him barking?"

Annie and Mitch both nodded.

"Anyway, in case you've forgotten, swimmer boy has an A meet in less than two hours." She poured herself a cup of steaming coffee from the automatic pot. "We've got to get there for warm-ups."

"Warm-ups!?" Mitch twirled off the stool. "I've got to get ready." He ran past his mother and to the stairs, rushing for the meet, but thinking about his friend.

What did I do to Josiah?

Mitch took the stairs two at a time.

I shouldn't have left him. How can I help Josiah if I never see him again?

Chapter 36

Sunday Morning. A Team.

Mrs. Burke sat in the van, nursing coffee in a thermal tumbler while Annie ate something green and gooey out of a paper cup. Mitch slid into the front seat with his swim bag.

"Want some?" Annie pushed the cup forward, into her brother's face. "It's extreme Jello. It's so hard you have to chew it."

"No thanks." Mitch wrinkled his nose.

Mrs. Burke and Annie sipped and slurped their cups all the way to the swimming pool. Mitch sat in silence. When they pulled into the parking lot, he opened the car door and hopped out. "I'll see you later."

"Good luck, honey!"

"Yeah, honey!" Annie mimicked.

Mitch tossed up a wave and ran through the guard gates to the poolside. Swimmers from the opposing team were already in the pool, churning up water. He stood on the platform and looked through the crowds, the scent of chlorine hitting his nostrils.

Where's Daryl?

The pool area was littered with team banners, portable tables, balloons, and volunteers in "Fear the Bug" T-shirts. Mitch struggled to find his coach and finally spied Daryl, who was surrounded by some of the younger Ladybug swimmers. They actually looked cute in their suits and swim trunks.

"Daryl!" He jogged up to his side. "I have a question for you. It's important."

Daryl looked up from the clipboard in his hands. A red and black whistle hung from his neck. "Hey buddy, what's up? You're not nervous are you?" He blew the whistle and the nine and ten year-old swimmers dove into the pool, launching into practice laps.

"No. But I need to know..."

"Whoa, guy, take a breath." Daryl put his hand on Mitch's shoulder. "Remember, breathe and relax. When you hold your breath you're wasting energy. Now breathe in..."

"What happens if the plan doesn't work?" Mitch squinted. "I mean, it works, then you realize it wasn't exactly the right plan…" Mitch's chest heaved as he finished his question.

"All plans are made to be tweaked." Daryl glanced back at the swimmers in the pool. "Champions often rethink their plans."

"Really?"

"Sure. Just take your time, refocus, and then go to the next level."

Mitch contemplated Daryl's response. "Refocus?"

Daryl nodded his head. "Do you think you could swim now?"

Mitch paused before he committed. "Yeah, I can swim now."

"Cool. Get in the pool and warm-up."

Without hesitation, Mitch bounded off the side of the pool and stretched into a long dive over an open lane, finally hitting the water in perfect form.

Refocus and go to the next level.

The clear water embraced his body. He swam nonstop without counting laps until Daryl called all swimmers out of the pool. The Mohicans regrouped by their table as the Ladybugs assembled at their own, chanting, "Fear the bug! Fear the bug!" The Mohicans responded with a competitive battle cry.

Standing by the huge Ladybug banner, Mitch saw Annie and his mother sitting up on Parents' Hill. They waved and screamed until he nodded acknowledgement.

Okay. Refocus. I've got to refocus. Now I've got to swim an A meet.

"Mitchell Burke!" Daryl was taking roll call.

Dear God, don't let me make an idiot of myself.

"Burke!"

"Here." Mitch felt the eyes of his team members on him.

"Sharon Carch!"

"Over here!" came a call from behind Mitch. He looked over his shoulder and noticed a new girl—short and trim—standing with the team.

She's kinda cute.

He smiled at her.

I can't believe I just did that.

She smiled back.

Mitch twisted around to face Daryl, who was plodding through roll call, joking with swimmers as he called their names.

Can we just get this over with?

He twitched and hopped on the grass to ease his nerves. Finally, the Clerk of Course shouted through the bullhorn to announce the start of the meet. Mitch quietly stood in his age group and waited until his event, boys 13-14 Freestyle, was called. Daryl walked him to his lane and gave him last-minute advice.

"Remember, relax your breathing, keep your hips on top of the water, arms as close to your body as possible, and kick rapidly with very little knee bend. You'll do great—you've got my word!"

The buzzer blared the start to Mitch's race.

I've got his word.

Adrenaline pushed his dive so far into the pool that he surfaced a full body-length ahead of his five competitors. He concentrated on his first breath so it wouldn't result in a gulp of chemical filled water.

The word. Keep your word. Everybody says keep your word.

His left arm led his body as he pulled the right around his ear and to the front.

Father Bob said 'You are your word.' Thomas Garrett said 'Honor thy word.'

Mitch's flutter kick propelled him through the first length of the race. He approached the wall smoothly, flipped, and gracefully pushed off into the second length. He sensed the current of another swimmer behind him, in the lane to his right. He pulled harder and sliced through the water, staying as close to the surface as possible, hips on top, arms to his sides.

I told Josiah I would get him out. I didn't keep my word.

He controlled his breath, reached the second wall, and flip-turned into the third length.

Refocus.

Mitch revved up his kicking, but kept his body steady.

I didn't keep my word to Josiah.

He pulled ahead of the opponent in the lane next to him.

I should've kept my word.

He lifted his shoulders higher and plowed through the water with increased power.

Dad said to beat her at her own game.

Mitch charged the wall and easily flip turned for the last 25-meter length.

I didn't beat her if she still has Josiah.

His elbows pitched high above his head before they served to slam his arms forward. His hands traveled by his body as he glided atop the water.

Go to the next level.

Mitch passed his closest opponent by a quarter pool length and smacked the wall to finish.

I'm going to get him out. I'm going to free Josiah.

Daryl and Mrs. Burke rushed past the timers to his lane. Mitch upped himself out of the pool in a rush of water, punched the air, and exclaimed, "I can do it!"

"*Can* do it?" screamed Daryl. "You did it, man. You're an All-Star!" He slapped Mitch on the back while the swimmers for the next event lined up. Daryl raised his stopwatch to show Mitch his All-Star time.

"All-Star. Wait until Dad hears!" Mrs. Burke hugged her wet son and wrapped a beach towel around his shoulders.

"All-Star?" Mitch looked around the pool deck and up Parents' Hill. "Where's Annie?"

"With the girls. Over there." His mom pointed as they walked off the pool deck and out of the way of the next event. Mitch looked over to see Annie, Meghan, and Sharon Carch waving from the snack bar, their arms full of bagels, donuts, and fruit cups.

"I need her help."

Chapter 37

Sunday Evening. Petey, the Ladybug, & Bed.

"Kids," Mrs. Burke swung her legs out of the van and onto the driveway, "this day did me a ton of good. I don't think we ever stayed at the pool so long…we ate all of our meals there!" She sat with the car door open to admire the lavender evening sky. "I can't wait to tell your father about it."

"I wish I could talk to Dad," Mitch whispered under his breath.

"Stop mumbling to yourself, Mr. Ladybug All-star. Even that new girl, Sharon, thought you looked great in the water today. She told me at the barbecue." Annie hopped from the van with her pool bag hanging on her shoulder. "I doubt she has seen the forest growing under your armpits, though," she said and slammed the door shut.

Mitch chuckled, pushed his door open with his sandaled feet, and stretched his upper body as he stood.

"Hey, Petey! What are you doing here?"

Petey sat on the stoop to the side door of the house. "Hi Mitch. Hi Mrs. Burke. Hi Annie."

"Hi Pete." Mrs. Burke strolled to the house and unlocked the door. "Would you like to come in?"

Mitch sat by Petey on the stairs while Annie swung from the porch post.

"No thank you. I just came by to tell Mitch that Fritzi came home."

"No, duh. The whole neighborhood could hear him!"

"Annie, knock it off!" Mitch scolded.

"We're happy to hear he's home, dear." Mrs. Burke entered the house. "Bed by 10, guys. I'm going to go read my book."

"Petey," Annie swung in his direction, "did you pray to St. Anthony? I bet you did."

Mitch scowled. "Annie, why don't you go inside with Mom?"

She relented. "I'm going to my room. You better come in soon if you want to talk to me."

"Fine."

Annie swung off the post and into the house, closing the door behind her.

"Mitch, I have something I want to give to you." Petey pulled his hand out of his pocket and produced a bright red—almost orange—ladybug.

"That's neat. But we should let the thing go free, don't you think?"

"I would, but her wing is broken. She can't fly. Someone will step on her or eat her if you don't take care of her."

Mitch scooped the ladybug out of Petey's hand and gently slid the wings apart with his forefinger. "Oh, I see."

ALMOST DEAD: One Unlucky Ladybug

"I'll tell you what." He dropped the ladybug into his wrinkled T-shirt pocket. "I'll keep her until her wing heals, then I'll let her go. Okay?"

Petey stood. "Thanks. I knew you could save her." He walked on the balls of his feet across the lawn to his house. Fritzi barked as he opened the door and entered. Mitch sighed and looked into his pocket crease at the half dead ladybug.

Great.

He walked into his own house and straight upstairs to Annie's room. Annie sat up in bed, Daryl's CD player and *Cosmic Comic* book 124 in her lap. When she saw Mitch, she pushed them both under her pillow and ironed the front of the pink pajamas she was wearing with her hands. "I thought you wanted to talk to me," she said.

"Annie, I'm worried about Josiah."

Don't scare her.

"I mean, I want to free him from Patty Cannon."

Annie scrunched her knees to her chest and rested her chin on the new platform. "But, you're free now. How are you going to do that?"

Mitch whispered, "I'm not exactly sure, but somehow I'm going to beat her at her own game."

"Yo, coo coo boy." She leaned forward over her knees. "You can't play with her anymore. You're out. Gone-zo. Free."

"Listen to me. I'm going to the next level." He ran his fingers through his hair. "I'm going to come in to your dream and deal with Patty head-on."

"What? What makes you think you can take over my dream?" She pulled her hair behind her head, balancing on her tailbone as her knees pulled to her chest. "I don't know if I want you to do that."

"Annie, if you don't let me, she might try to hurt you, too."

"But, she can't."

"Why not? She hurt Josiah…and, she took Fritzi."

Annie's hair fell over her knees as she hugged them tighter. "I don't know.

You got Fritzi back…"

"But, I'm not there anymore." Mitch paused. "Don't you see? You're on your own."

"Why do you think you can enter one of my dreams?"

"I can do it. I know I can. Remember your peanuts? I took them into my dream with me. I wished them into my dream."

Her blue eyes widened. "No way."

"And then, I ate them while I was in jail and tossed the bag into the hallway. The bag stayed in my dream. It didn't come back with me."

"I *told* you it would work!"

"And you were right, it did." He pulled his feet up onto the bed. "I can do this, Annie. It's the only way."

"This is scary. What if she gets really angry? What if she comes after both of us?"

"Patty likes her games, right?"

Annie nodded while she chewed her blond hair and lay down on her side.

"And, she takes them seriously, right?"

"Right."

"That's all you need to know."

"Mitch!"

"Trust me. I'm going to end Patty's game." Mitch lay down on her bed, his head at the footboard and his legs alongside his sister's back. "I promise."

Annie settled back and pulled the sheets under her nose. "Are you going to sleep in those?" She mumbled into the sheets. "Your T-shirt and shorts?"

"Quiet. Make sure you're touching a part of me."

"This is weird." She put her arm behind her side and over Mitch's leg. He tucked his arms in to his chest.

"Now, remember your relaxation CDs. Close your eyes and inhale."

Annie closed her eyes and inhaled deeply.

"Think of me in your dream. In the meadow."

Mitch closed his eyes and relaxed his own breathing.

"Think of me with you. At your side when you see Patty."

Annie inhaled and exhaled, until she fell asleep.

"Now, think of Patty's surprise when she sees me."

Dear God, please help me keep my word to Josiah.

He inhaled and exhaled.

And, to Annie.

Chapter 38

Back in the Meadow.

"So, Mitchey-Boy. I knew you'd come back to Patty."

Mitch looked up from the meadow floor to see Patty Cannon standing over him, her hands on her hips, dried blood clotted on her thick arms. He sat up, rested back on his elbows, and yelled, "I'm free!"

Annie, sitting alongside Mitch, swept the grass off her pink pajamas. "Hello."

Patty spoke to Mitch. "Your mine now that you're here."

He looked down at his T-shirt, shorts, and bare feet and patted his shirt pocket, noticing Petey's ladybug made the trip as well. "Look." He pulled the T-shirt away from his chest. "Twenty-first century clothes."

Silence hung over the hot, hazy day.

"You don't have me, Patty. Annie brought me here and I'm free."

Annie smiled.

Patty pitched her head back, tossing her mane off her sweaty shoulders, and paced in front of the brother and sister. Josiah hobbled out of the woods, supporting himself with a knobby stick.

"What did you do to Josiah?" Mitch sprang to his feet. "What did you do to him?"

Patty roared a massive laugh. "You think you can escape my meadow, run from my men, manipulate your sister, steal the dog, cross over into freedom… and expect your friend here to be safe?" She pointed to the weakened Josiah and then at Mitch. "You sneaking snitch. What kind of family *are* you?"

Annie stood next to Mitch and whimpered, "She's scaring me."

"Don't be scared. Don't let her get to you." He put his arm around Annie's shoulder.

"Ah. Isn't that sweet, now? Big brother caring for his sister." Patty rolled her head on her shoulders, cracking her neck. First once, then twice. She stomped toward Josiah. "Too bad he didn't care enough for your sake!" She reached Josiah, grabbed his ear and pulled him, wincing in pain, to where Mitch and Annie stood. Blood trickled from the top of Josiah's ear, to his lobe.

"Let him go!" Mitch screamed.

"This is my meadow and I do as I please." She shoved Josiah to the ground, bent over, and grabbed his stick. "My meadow, my rules!" She rapped the stick against the palm of her own large hand.

Annie clutched Mitch. The heavy heat of the meadow sank onto his skin and beads of sweat boiled under his T-shirt.

She's vulnerable. I know she's vulnerable.

"I have an idea." Mitch boldly addressed Patty.

"An idea, now? What makes you think I'm looking for an idea from you?" Patty waved the stick at Josiah. "Ideas aren't what I'm looking for."

"What, what if we play a game?"

"A game?" Her black eyes flashed. "You come back to play a game?"

Mitch hesitated before he spoke. "I want to play a game for Josiah's freedom."

Patty wrinkled her brow and frowned. She furled a gob of spit at Mitch's feet. "You know I take my games seriously."

"If I win, you let Josiah go and stop trying to snare Annie."

"I always win." Patty rubbed spittle from her chin. "What do I get when I win?"

Mitch swallowed. "If you win, you get me."

"Mitch!" Annie tugged his shirt.

"No!" screamed Josiah from the ground. "Jes' leave me be and save yerselves."

Patty tilted her head to her shoulder and smiled. "Winner takes all. I get all of you."

Mitch motioned for Annie to go to Josiah, who now huddled on the ground. She knelt by the boy, but never took her eyes off her brother.

"How do I know you'll keep your word?" Mitch asked.

"You know damn well I keep my word when it comes to games. Nobody plays with a cheater!"

"Okay." Mitch ran his fingers through his hair. "Two out of three, winner takes all."

"One game only." She stamped her foot. "Or no game."

He rubbed the sweat from his face over his dry lips, his hand landing on his pocket. "Okay, but then I pick the game."

Patty paced around Mitch, slapping the large stick against her palm. He could smell her sweat and studied the beaten ground she walked on, waiting for her reaction. She stopped in front of him, struck a huge smile, and bellowed, "So, what's the game?"

I can do this.

"The game is Pigeon Flies."

"Ha!" Patty tossed her head back. "You know I'm quite comfortable with that game now, don't you?"

Mitch nodded.

"Then we'll play my favorite, Pigeon Flies."

"Mitchey, please jes' go." Josiah pleaded.

Mitch shook his head and sat cross-legged at his sister's side, whispering, "Make sure you keep a hand on me. Touch me." Annie rested her hand on her brother's back.

Patty sat cross-legged across from Mitch, Annie, and Josiah. "Remember the rules. First, put your pointer finger on my knee."

Mitch squared his shoulders. "I call the game. You called the last one." He bit his lip. "That was your rule."

Beat her at her own game.

Patty leaned back and raised her eyebrows. "Now, now. Ain't you got a fine memory? So be it. You call."

Mitch extended his left pointer finger and laid it on his knee. "Okay, you have to put your finger on my knee."

Patty extended her finger and dropped it on Mitch's knee.

"Next," Mitch continued, "when I call out the name of an animal that flies, you raise that finger to the sky." He raised his own shaking finger to demonstrate. "If you don't raise your finger, or if you raise your finger when I call an animal that doesn't fly, you lose."

"You remember our last game, Mitchey-boy? You really lost that one. Ha!" She snorted a chuckle.

Mitch frowned and called, "Pigeon!"

Patty snorted louder and raised her finger to the sky. "Maybe you'll want to ask Josiah about your family tree."

What?

He hesitated. "Dog!"

Patty's finger pressed into Mitch's knee. "Oh yes. You both have a *dog* in the family. That's correct."

Confused, Mitch glanced at Josiah, who was rubbing sweat from his face. He looked back at Patty.

"Snake!"

"You definitely share a *snake*. Right, Josiah?"

Patty's finger pressed deeper into Mitch's knee and Annie's hand deeper into his back.

"Ya keep quiet!" Josiah blurted at Patty.

"Why don't ya tell Mitchey-boy the truth about your grandpappy?" Patty curled her lips into a smile.

What is going on?

"Mosquito!" Mitch called.

Patty's finger flew to the sky and then back to Mitch's knee.

"Ooh, too nervous are you to tell the truth, Josiah?"

"Leave them be! Ya have me, ain't that enough?" the boy yelled.

She's ruining it. She's taking control.

"Josiah," Annie whispered, "What is she talking about?"

"Robin!"

Patty pointed to the sky, "Too easy, Mitchey." She rested her finger back on his knee. "Go ahead, boy. Tell them you're a relation, why don't you? That way, I don't look like such an evil witch for keeping you."

Mitch eyed Josiah, sweat dripping from his tight hair.

Take control.

"Squirrel!"

"You know damn well some squirrels fly." Her finger shot up, and then back to his knee.

Mitch felt his T-shirt pocket with his right hand.

"Crow!"

"Make them harder," Annie pleaded in his ear.

Patty's finger rose to the sky and thumped back on Mitch's knee.

It's time.

Mitch reached into his pocket and removed the ladybug Petey had given him. He rolled the injured bug into his palm and extended his hand in front of Patty.

"This ladybug."

"Listen to your sister, Mitchey-boy. Make the game harder or else we'll be sharing eternity. Isn't that right, Josiah?"

Josiah avoided Patty's glare and leaned against Annie.

Mitch clenched his teeth and pointed to the ladybug. "I said, *this* ladybug!"

Patty snickered. "Everyone knows ladybugs can fly." She pointed to the sky.

Mitch flew to his feet, Annie's hand gripping his ankle. "Not this one!"

He dropped the ladybug from his hand and let it fall to the ground. Once it hit, it rolled to its feet, its broken wing extended in an awkward side angle. "This one has a broken wing and can't fly!"

Patty roared, "You tricked me!"

Chapter 39

Last Time in the Meadow.

Annie leaned forward and scooped up the bug.

"Mitch. Mitch!" Josiah screamed. "What's happening to me?" Josiah's hands shook uncontrollably. He put them out for Mitch to see.

"You tricked me!" Patty sprang up from the ground, her fists clenched at her sides.

"Are they tingling, Josiah? Can you feel them tingle?"

Josiah rose to his feet without the help of a stick, his hands stretched out at his sides. His entire body visibly trembled. "My whole body is set to tingle. What do I do?"

"Give me that bug!" Patty tried to snatch the ladybug from Annie. "I'll show you that ladybugs fly!"

Mitch grabbed Annie's arm and pulled her to her feet. "Annie, hold on. Don't let me go and don't give her Petey's ladybug." He turned to Josiah. "Run Josiah, run away. You're a free boy!"

Patty lunged at Josiah. "Don't you go anywhere, boy. You belong to me!"

Josiah hopped backwards, out of her reach. "I feel, I feel different!" He ran backwards, his knees pumping to his chest. "My legs don't hurt no more!"

"You're mine!"

"He's free, Patty." Mitch faced her.

"His grandpappy killed my pappy!" Patty screamed.

"That was *my* Grandfather Lawrence, not his," said Mitch.

Patty whipped around to face Mitch and Annie, "Your grandpappy <u>was</u> his grandpappy!" She jabbed a fist toward Josiah, who had stopped moving and stood, his hands on his head.

"What?" Mitch, holding Annie's hand, addressed Josiah. "What is she talking about?"

Josiah now held his head in his hands. "Yer Grandpappy Lawrence was my pappy's pappy. He was my Grandpappy Lawrence, too."

"We're related?"

"He's a bastard child!" Patty paced and spat at the same time.

Josiah continued, "Grandmammy worked in the big house and Grand-pappy was a widower at the time. Seems Grandpappy took a likin' to Grand-mammy...and my pappy was born in the quarters right there behind the big house."

"You mean, we have the same *white* great whatever grandfather?"

Josiah nodded.

"Why didn't you tell me?"

"I didn't want ya comin' back on my account. Jes' cuz I'm family."

"But I gave you my word I would."

"I didn't count on that. People come back fer family, usually not fer a stranger."

"Yes they do. All those people helped me—a stranger."

"You used foolery to trick me!" Patty swung her arms in the air. "He was mine!"

"He isn't yours to have." Mitch spun around and, still holding Annie's hand, stepped back from Patty's large figure. "Josiah, you're fee. You just gotta go!"

Josiah smiled, nodded, and ran to the woods, his arms and legs gracefully carrying him out of sight.

Run Josiah. Run.

"He was mine!"

"Patty," interjected Annie, "please don't yell."

"Argh!" Patty leapt at Annie.

"She's not afraid of you, Pirate Patty." Mitch planted his feet firmly between Patty and Annie. "And neither am I."

Chapter 40
Monday Early Morning.

Mitch woke, still tucked in at the foot of Annie's bed. He opened his eyes.

I'm out.

He looked down at Annie, curled up like a baby with her hands in fists, pressed against her chest. Then, he lifted his groggy head enough to look at the digital clock on her bedside table. The yellow squares blared, "4:15 A. M."

We're here, we're okay.

Annie slept soundly, breathing steadily and calmly. Mitch patted her knee, but she didn't wake.

I better let her sleep.

He plumped the stuffed bear he was using for a pillow and lay his head back down.

What happens if I go back to sleep?

The numbers on the clock changed to "4:16 A.M." and Mitch closed his eyes. He inhaled and then exhaled. By 4:17 A.M., he was back asleep.

Chapter 41

Monday Morning. To The Library.

The sun blasted into Annie's bedroom window, sending Mitch to pull the stuffed bear over his eyes.

Why does she keep her drapes open?

He rolled over to face the wall and stretched his legs all the way to Annie's headboard, pushing her pillow along the way. His sister was already out of bed.

"Hey!"

Mitch sat up under the top bunk.

I didn't dream about Patty Cannon.

He swung his legs out of the bed and sat hunched over the side. The clock read, "8:15 A.M."

I don't think I dreamt about anything.

Mitch jumped and punched the air with both fists. "It worked!" He bolted from Annie's room, down the stairs two at time, and skidded into the kitchen. His mom and Annie were eating breakfast at the kitchen table, Mrs. Burke sitting in her work clothes and Annie in her swimsuit. Fritzi was barking in the Kimmel's front yard.

"Aren't you full of energy this morning!" Mrs. Burke greeted her son. "Sit and listen to the wild dream your sister had last night."

Mitch patted Annie on her back. She giggled, exposing the oatmeal that oozed between her teeth.

"Anna Maria, stop that!"

"What was the dream about?" Mitch sat at his place, marked by the folded obituaries.

His mother pointed at her daughter. "This one dreamt that you were chased by an evil woman and had to escape on the Underground Railroad to freedom."

Mitch leaned over the obituaries and raised his eyebrows at his sister, who swung both arms in the air.

"She was about to be captured, but you saved her, and the woman disappeared forever."

"Really?" Mitch drawled.

"Boo-ya, really!" Annie danced from the waist up in her chair.

Mitch shook his head. "Speaking of Underground Railroad, Mom, can I skip swim practice today to finish my report at the library?"

Mrs. Burke stood from the table and put her bowl in the sink. "Hmm."

"Please? I think I need one more day of research." He rolled the newspaper and casually swatted a fly, which escaped down the hallway.

"What will Daryl think?"

"I'll explain it to him. Maybe I can swim doubles tomorrow."

Mrs. Burke relented and, ten minutes later, the three settled into the van, Annie in the front seat. Mrs. Burke wheeled the car out of the driveway and onto the street towards the library.

Annie turned to face Mitch in the back. "I have a present for you." She thrust her arm in between the seats and pushed her fist toward Mitch's face. She released her fingers one by one and exposed the upturned palm of her hand.

"Petey's ladybug!" Mitch cried.

Annie nodded her head. "Watch this." She nudged the bug with her finger. It opened its red wings to expose the black ones underneath.

"The wing isn't crooked anymore," Mitch whispered.

Annie nudged it again and it responded by flying off her hand and into the back seat. They watched as it flew from seat to seat, armrest to armrest.

It can fly.

Mitch lowered his window. The ladybug found its way to the opening, steadied itself on the window frame, and flew into the breeze. Annie turned back around in her seat and Mitch shut the window.

Wow.

Moments later, the Burke van pulled steadily into the Clean Drinking library parking lot. "Bye, guys." Mitch got out of the car and entered the library lobby, where a rush of cool air greeted him. He pulled his backpack up on his shoulder and turned left to the volunteer desk.

"Good morning, Mrs. Sharpe." Mitchell plopped his backpack on the desk in front of the docent.

"Please get that off my desk, young man." Mrs. Sharpe looked up and over her glasses to address Mitch as he removed the bag. "Oh, it's you, Mr. Burke."

"Yes, ma'am."

The squat, chubby lady took off her glasses and let them hang at her neck. "What can I do for you today, Mr. Burke?"

"Ma'am, you may call me Mitchell."

"Oh, yes indeed. Mitchell. What can I do for you today?" She fiddled with six colored felt tip markers that lined her desk.

"Well, ma'am. I'm finishing the research for the project I'm working on…"

"Yes, on the Underground Railroad in Maryland, as I recall."

"Yes, ma'am. That's right."

"You mean, 'That's correct.'"

"Yes, ma'am. That's correct." Mitch fidgeted with the backpack strap. "And I'm almost finished…"

"You already said that. That you're almost finished."

"Yes, ma'am. So, now I need…"

"More time on the Internet?" Mrs. Sharpe scowled.

"Well, actually, ma'am, I was wondering if you could recommend a good book on the history of slavery on Maryland's Eastern Shore?"

"Oh, of course. I would love to recommend one!" She turned to her desk computer and fumbled over the keys. "Let me just find our historical regional reading list. Oh dear, where did I file that?"

"Mrs. Sharpe? Maybe I can email my dad while you look." Mitch leaned forward over her desk. "May I use the Internet?"

"Oh certainly. Certainly, dear." Mrs. Sharpe placed the glasses on her nose and returned her attention to the drawer. "I'll fetch you when I find the list, dear. Do tell your father what marvelous work you're doing on your project."

Mitch smiled and ambled to the computer room, where he chose the first available terminal, under the buzz of the fluorescent lights.

"Hi, Mitch." Sharon Carch smiled from the terminal next to his.

He hopped a step backwards. "What are you doing here? I mean, why aren't you at practice?"

"School project. Today's the only morning this week I could do research." She pulled one leg under her bottom. "I bet you're doing the same." Sharon smiled and looked back to her screen.

She really is cute.

Mitch sat and logged on to his email.

Ding!

I've got mail.

He opened his inbox to find six messages from his dad: Friday 10:48 P.M., Friday 11:59 P.M., Saturday 5:10 A.M., Sunday 2:00 A.M., Sunday 11:23 P.M., and Monday 9:15 A.M.

Monday!

Mitch looked at his watch.

9:16. Dad's on the computer!
He rushed to open the last note.

> **Mitch: Any progress? Please answer me. I'm worried about you.**
> **Love, Dad**

He sat straight in his chair, hit "reply," and typed furiously.

> **Dad! Are you still there? I'm free. I made it to Pennsylvania and I'm free! Why didn't you tell me Josiah is a cousin? Oh well, we're all free!**
>
> **Write back.**
> **Mitch**

Mitch sent his message, sat back in his chair, and closed his eyes. His heart raced, so he concentrated on his breath and inhaled deeply.
Dear God, this has been exhausting…
He closed his eyes.
…but, I wasn't chased by dogs, beaten, or sold from my family.
He stretched his arms in the air and brought them back to his sides, looking at his hands as they rested in his lap.
Imagine what the real slaves lived through.
Ding!
Mitch pounded open a message from his father.

> **Son, I am so proud of you. I knew you could do it. I'll explain your distant grandfather's story later. We'll take a long walk and talk this over when I get back. Most importantly, you should be proud of yourself.**
>
> **BTW: You're the first to hear…we might not have to stay on. There's a chance our unit will come home in 3 weeks. I can't wait to be with all of you. Tell Mom I'll phone her later.**
>
> **I'm so relieved…**
>
> **I love you,**
> **Dad**

Mitch sprang from his chair. "He's coming home!"

Sharon peeked over her computer. "Your dad?"

"Yes!" He plopped back down in his chair and instinctively glanced over at the volunteer desk.

Mrs. Sharpe stood, her left forefinger in a "shh" to her lips, and her right hand extended in a "thumbs up." He smiled and sent her a thumbs-up in return.

Mitch ran his fingers through his uncombed hair and closed his eyes.

Dear God, I did it.

He refocused.

Thank you.

"I looked at my hands, to see if I was the same person now that I was free. There was such a glory over everything; the sun came like gold through the trees, and over de fields, and I felt like I was in heaven."

-Harriet Tubman

Bibliography

Agle, Nan Hayden, *Free To Stay: The True Story of Eliza Benson and the Family She Stood by for Three Generations* (Fruitland: Arcadia Enterprises, Inc., 2000).

Appelbaum, Stanley, ed., *Henry Wadsworth Longfellow Favorite Poems* (Mineola: Dover Publications, Inc., 1992).

Appelbaum, Stanley, and Philip Smith, ed., *Frederick Douglass: The Narratives of Frederick Douglass* (Mineola: Dover Publications, Inc., 1995).

Ball, Edward, *Slaves in the Family* (New York: The Ballantine Publishing Group, 1998).

Berlin, Ira, Marc Favreau, and Steven F. Miller, ed., *Remembering Slavery: African Americans Talk About Their Personal Experiences of Slavery and Freedom* (New York: The New Press, in conjunction with the Library of Congress, 1998).
Biographies of Samuel Burris, Thomas Garrett, and William Still (http://www.whispersofangels.com).

Bordewich, Fergus M., *Bound For Canaan: The Epic Story of the Underground Railroad, America's First Civil Rights Movement* (New York: Harper Paperbacks, 2006).

de Capua, Sarah E., *Abolitionists: A Force for Change* (Mankato: The Child's World, 2002).

Carbone, Elisa, *Stealing Freedom* (New York: Random House, 2000).

Delaware State Archives, *Slavery Papers*, Legal documents related to the treatment of slaves living in the State of Delaware (http://archives.delaware.gov).

DiFillipo, Thomas J., *History and Develpment of Upper Darby*, 2nd Edition (Upper Darby: Upper Darby Historical Society, 1992).

Drew, Benjamin, *The Refugee: Narratives of Fugitive Slaves in Canada* (Boston: John P. Jewett & Co., 1856).

Hansen, Joyce, and Gary McGowan, *Freedom Roads: Searching for the Underground*

Railroad (Chicago: Cricket Books, 2003).

Hurmence, Belinda, ed., *My Folks Don't Want Me To Talk About Slavery: Personal Accounts of Slavery in North Carolina* (Winston-Salem: John F. Blair, Publisher, 1984).

Gorrell, Gena K., *North Star to Freedom: The Story of the Underground Railroad* (New York: Delacorte Press, 1996).

Jones, Edward P., *The Known World* (New York: Amistad, 2003).

Lawson, Kate Clifford, *Bound For The Promised Land: Harriet Tubman: Portrait of an American Hero* (New York: One World/Ballantine, 2004).

Lengyel, Jeff, prod. and dir., *Underground Railroad*, 95 min., A&E Home Video, 1999, DVD.

Loewen, James W., *Lies Across America: What Our Historic Sites Get Wrong* (New York: Touchstone, by arrangement with The New Press, 1999).

The Long Road to Freedom: An Anthology of Black Music, Harry Belafonte and David Belafonte, Buddha Records, CD, 2001.

McMullan, Kate, *The Story of Harriet Tubman* (New York: Bantam Doubleday Dell Books for Young Readers, 1991).

Mescher, Michael, and Virginia Burke, *Mid-Nineteenth Century Parlor Games* (Burke: Nature's Finest, 1998).

Mitchell, Patricia B., *Plantation Row Slave Cabin Cooking: The Roots of Soul Food* (Chatham: Mitchells Publications, 1998).

Narrative and Confessions of Lucretia P. Cannon (New York: Printed for the publishers, 1841).

Norman, Michael, and Beth Scott, *Haunted Heritage* (New York: Tom Dougherty Associates, LLC, 2002).

Ochoa, Anna, ed., "The Record: The Black Experience in America 1619-1979," *The Wilmington Delaware Sunday News Journal*, February 18, 1979, Special supplement sponsored by The National Association for the Advancement of Colored People, the Anti-Defamation League of B'Nai B'rith, and the National Council for the Social Studies.

Patty Cannon, obit., *Delaware Gazette*, May 19, 1829.

Perry, Mark, *Lift Up Thy Voice: The Grimke Family's Journey from Slaveholders to Civil Rights Leaders* (New York: Viking, 2001).

Stowe, Harriet Beecher, *Uncle Tom's Cabin or Life Among the Lowly* (Cambridge: The Riverside Press, 1851).

Townsend, George Alfred, *The Entailed Hat, or Patty Cannon's Times* (Vienna: Nanticoke Books, 1884).

Truth, Sojourner, *Narrative of Sojourner Truth* (Mineola: Dover Thrift Editions, 1997).

Blockson, Charles L., "The Underground Railroad," *National Geographic*, Volume 166, No. 1 (July 1984).

U.S. Department of the Interior, National Park Service, Division of Publications, *Underground Railroad, Official National Park Handbook, No. 156*, 1998.

U.S. Department of the Interior, National Park Service, Management Concepts/ Environmental Assessment, Denver Service Center, *Underground Railroad, Special Resource Study*, 1995.

Washington, Booker T., *Up From Slavery: An Autobiography* (New York: Doubleday, Page & Co., 1901).

Acknowledgments

Freestyle sprung from a moment of inspiration, followed by years of effort, support, and Ladybug swim meets. Thank you, Tony Cohen, for introducing me to our bad lady, Patty Cannon. Thanks to my coveted writing community: Mary Quattlebaum, for launching me; Linda Zuckerman, for giving me a reality check; Treetops, critique group extraordinaire, for keeping me on track; and Traci Grigg, who read every word, many times. Cynthia Snyder, of the Newcastle Court House Museum was instrumental in providing Courthouse and period information, and Jolie McCathran of the Sandy Spring Friends Meeting corrected my "Quaker-speak." Neither of you had to log the time that you did. Thank you. Most of all, I have my family to thank—Mom, Dad, Tillie, and Poppop—for believing in me. Blood and in-laws, for your unscripted joy at my publication. For my friends I'm fortunate. George, my #1 fan; Gracie, my #1 reader; and Cole and Ava, for all of those road trips. I love you.